THE
AMERICAN
SWEENEY TODD

FROM THE #1 BESTSELLING *WALL STREET JOURNAL* AUTHOR OF
AFTER MIDNIGHT IN THE GARDEN OF GOOD AND EVIL:

THE
AMERICAN
SWEENEY TODD

ELIOT NESS'S TOUGHEST CASE

A NOVEL
BY MARILYN J. BARDSLEY

Eliot Ness, Attribution: public domain image
courtesy of WikiMedia Commons

DARKHORSE MULTIMEDIA, INC.

First Edition
Paperback ISBN: 978-0-9983516-0-5
Kindle ISBN: 978-0-9983516-1-2

Contents

Dedication

For Elliott, Rachael, Ulla, Jay, Devon, and Jordyn

Acknowledgments

I THANK ALL OF YOU WHO have taken the time to read this story. My hope is that you can appreciate the complexity of the talented, hard-working man who fell so far and so fast from the fulfillment of his dreams. It was a tragedy, not only for his victims but for his family.

This novel could not have been written without Walter Bell and Elliott Bardsley. Walter, my co-investigator, kept us safe during the years we tracked down the leads, finally uncovering the identity of the man Eliot Ness kept secret for more than thirty years. Elliott was the inspiration and advisor for a number of scenes that were difficult for me to write.

I am also deeply indebted to Steve Bennett and his talented team at AuthorBytes for the enormous effort put forth to create our books, websites, and media. AuthorBytes' vast experience has liberated me from managing all the activities necessary to success-fully publish a book.

Prologue

THE MOONLIGHT CAST DEEP SHADOWS OVER the ancient metalwork of the bridge. A light rain had begun to fall, generating a rank and unwholesome smell from the rusted tracks below.

Time seemed to have stopped in Kingsbury Run. The vast changes the city had seen over the years had barely touched the ugly ravine that cut a long, jagged wound across more than fifty blocks of Cleveland's east side—an open sore festering with the decay of industrial and human debris. Mountains of sand and gravel, whose ownership and use were obscure. Gaping corpses of machinery stripped of all dignity and purpose. Monuments to technology discarded, choked by the overgrowth of stunted sumac and tall grass.

It was all but silent now that the Great Depression was a distant memory. Gone were the hordes of homeless creatures who had wandered the lonely paths of the Run, huddling under the pathetic shelter of the bridge, finding refuge in corrugated metal and cardboard shacks. Hundreds of the unemployed had poured into the city hoping to find work in the mills. As these unfortunates obliterated their pain in pint bottles and begged for food, they became the prey of the dark presence that stalked them.

The city had a frenzied fascination with this grim wasteland. Thousands of spectators watched for hours as police dredged the oily, stagnant pools for pieces of his victims. Reporters fed voraciously on each murder, whipping the city into a panic. Eliot Ness, who had been hired to clean up the massive corruption in the city's police force, was compelled to divert his attention to a taunting serial killer. Three years with no resolution, the unsolved case tarnished the reputation of the famous young lawman.

Now, many decades later, the man who bragged that he was the American Sweeney Todd, comes to life again through his journals—a surgeon with great promise who fell prey to his inner demons and lost it all.

THE JOURNALS:

THE FALL

MARCH 22, 1935

I missed yesterday, and what a black day it was, but I haven't missed a day since St. Paddy's last year. Of course, I don't have to apologize to myself, but I feel so much better when I write every day. I may be the only voice of reason left in my life.

I spent last night here in the office on the couch. I just couldn't stomach going home and listening to her infernal bleating. At least here I can have a couple of drinks and sort things out in peace.

I've spent a lot of time today trying to understand Mary. Women are such flawed, irrational creatures. She keeps whining that I should spend more time at home, but then she goes out of her way to make me miserable the moment I walk in the door. Always on me about how much I drink, making me so tense that I just want to crawl inside that bottle of whiskey and go to sleep. Now, Mary is fairly intelligent, as women go, and we've talked about this crazy behavior of hers on numerous occasions, but nothing changes. In fact, it's becoming more acute. I can't see living this way much longer.

The night before last was an exquisite example. As usual, I went out with the lads for a few drinks after work. With the kind of pressure I'm under at the hospital every day, I need to let off some steam for an hour or so before I go home.

I made a special point of getting home before seven-thirty, so I could spend some time with the boys before they went to bed. So, what does that crazy, fat-ass beast do? She sends them to bed early, around seven o'clock. Why? Because she invited that goddamn Polish priest of hers to talk to me about my drinking. I was really mad. Jaworski or whatever the hell his name is, was sitting in the living room with a cup of coffee. Sonofabitch doesn't drink at all. Any decent Irish priest would have been drinking some whiskey. If she was going to ruin my evening, she could have at least asked an Irish priest over. Lord knows there are enough of them at St. Tim's.

My son, he says. Bastard can't be more than a year older than me, and he calls me son. You're making your family suffer. He had this agonized expression on his face as though I just backed the car out over his foot.

Suffer? I asked him. Look around at this house in a good neighborhood. Look at the new furniture. Look at Mary. Does she look underfed? If you want to see suffering, come with me to the hospital. I'll show you some real suffering. And what about a third of the men in this city who can't find any work? Go downtown sometime and watch the bums eating out of garbage cans. That's suffering. My wife and sons aren't suffering.

If anyone is miserable in this family, I told him, it's me. Every day I work with the sick and dying and then come home to a wife who does nothing but bitch at me. Try it sometime.

Well, he wasn't about to listen to my side of the story. Mary had already pumped him full of her lies. While he went on with his pious bullshit, I stepped into the kitchen and poured myself a drop of refreshment. With my glass in hand, I listened quietly for fifteen minutes and then I asked him very politely if he was through. I had some important work to do, and I thought it was time for him to leave.

The bastard had the nerve to tell me he wasn't going to leave my house until I agreed to get some treatment for my "problem" as he called it. I told him that from where I was standing, I had two problems, the solution for which were divorce and excommunication.

I suppose I could have just picked him up and thrown him out on the porch, but Mary would never have let me hear the end of it. So, I put on my hat and coat and started to leave. You don't have to go, I told him. You can stay all night. Sleep on the couch or even in my bed. Take it from me, I assured him. There's no danger of losing your celibacy sleeping next to my wife.

I went back to Dugan's in the old neighborhood and felt better the moment I walked in. Now Dugan's leaves a lot to be desired in a tavern. It's drafty. The seats are hard and uncomfortable, and the whiskey is somewhat watered, but it's more like a home to me than the house I just left. Nobody to count how many drinks I have. Nobody to fuss if I drop an ash on the floor. Nobody to frown when my language gets rowdy.

Bertie and Driscoll were still there, and of course, Patty was behind the bar. They were happy to see me back and sympathetically listened as I told them how I was driven from my house by a priest and an inconsiderate wife. Just think how many times the hallowed walls of Dugan's have heard that story from generations of miserable husbands.

Well, we sang, and we joked. I even danced with Patty when her father went out for a few minutes. I guess we closed the place up. I don't remember.

But, I got to the hospital yesterday morning in time for my eight o'clock. Although, today I wished to bloody hell I had slept right through it. To be perfectly honest, I wasn't in my best form.

It was a simple hysterectomy. Everything was going fine when all of a sudden the scalpel slipped and cut the uterine artery. Jesus Christ! What a goddamn mess. Blood spurting out everywhere. And what does that moron, Helen, do? She panics. She freezes. I'm shouting orders to her, and she's moving around in slow motion with her big, ugly frog eyes bulging. Why is it I get stuck with the least competent nurse in the whole hospital? No thanks to Helen, I stopped the hemorrhaging and went on with the procedure.

Helen, that redheaded whore, must have run right into Mullen's office as soon as the operation was over. He barged in while I was washing up. I've never seen the old windbag so red in the face.

You're drunk, he said. I won't stand for that in this hospital. I protested, but he didn't believe me. I wasn't drunk. Not seriously drunk. Not too drunk to do a simple hysterectomy. It was an accident. Could have happened to anyone, but he told me to get out. Suspended me until further notice.

I tried to talk quietly and rationally to him. Explained I'd been up all night, and that's why I looked like hell. Hung over a bit but not drunk. I love it, how he takes the word of some idiot nurse over a surgeon. For five years, I've worked in that hospital with never a blemish on my name, but then he's never liked me. I'm so much smarter than he is. And so much taller. I'd like to cut his goddamn throat and watch him bleed to death.

What pisses me off the most is that I'm going to have to crawl back to him. I can't afford a suspension for long. Not with the way Mary spends my money.

Fortunately, I didn't have any other operations scheduled for yesterday. I came back to my office and saw several patients. I can't imagine what they thought, considering how mad I was.

The minute the last patient left, I pulled out my emergency bottle and poured myself a stiff one. All I could think about was revenge. What can I do to Mullens to fix that bastard permanently? A dozen crazy ideas came into my head, but I didn't think any of them would actually work.

I slept for a couple of hours and went back to Dugan's. Bertie and Driscoll were waiting for me to find out what the hell happened.

The whole hospital had buzzed all day about it. As usual, Helen had exaggerated everything way out of proportion. Driscoll heard I had gone after her with a scalpel. In retrospect, I probably should have.

I stayed there until Driscoll left around nine. Then I went over to the diner and got myself a roast beef sandwich. I seriously thought about going home, but why subject myself to any more abuse? I'd had enough for one day. Another night on the couch in the serenity of my office.

MARCH 23, 1935

Time hangs very heavy on my hands. That's not good for me. When I have nothing to do, I drink and smoke too much. I should be working. Every day of my goddamn life, I've worked. Tomorrow I must force myself to talk to that sonofabitch Mullens and get myself reinstated. It's just so very hard for me to humble myself to that senseless piece of dog shit, but if I don't do something soon, I'll be the one to suffer.

What really galls me is he knows he has me completely under his control because I need to send my patients to a hospital nearby. I can't very well ask people to go way across town for operations. I just can't believe after all these years struggling for financial independence, I've gotten myself under the thumb of a tyrant like Mullens.

I had to get my mind on something else, so I decided to go over to Agnes's. I tried to call her, but the phone was cut off. Things must be harder for her than I realized. Everything is getting worse. So many men out of work. Every day I read about another company going out of business. At least that's not one of my worries. As long as people get sick, I'll always have an income. Even so, bad times have hit me too. Lots of people pay slow, sometimes not at all. And they're putting off operations until they have enough money.

When I got to Agnes's house, Lee was at the tavern. I get the feeling he spends a lot of time there lately. But Agnes, unlike my wife, doesn't complain about it. Fortunately, she's doing some bookkeeping work on the side that will get her phone connected next week.

I was upset by how Agnes looked. So washed out and fragile. She used to be so pretty. I told her I wanted her to come into the office as soon as she could, so I can find out what's wrong. She said she had just gotten over a bad cold, but I still want to take a look at her.

I warned her if she didn't come by in the next few days, I'd bring my black bag out and give her the full treatment right there. What's the sense of having a brother who's a doctor if you don't use him when you're sick?

She looks a lot like Mama now. I'd never noticed the strong resemblance before. My memory of Mama is so dim. All I have left of her are a couple of photographs. Maybe Agnes's likeness to her is what worries me so much. Mama was just about Agnes's age when she died. Jesus, I hope nothing happens to Agnes. She's the only person in the world who cares whether I'm alive or dead.

I feel good when we're together. It's just we two little lost kids again. That's what Sis used to call us when we were growing up. We were always together. Totally dependent on each other.

I'll never forget when Agnes climbed on the top of McDermott's garage to rescue the cat. Once she was up there, she was afraid to come down. We were so worried old man McDermott would be mad at us for climbing on his garage that I didn't go for help.

Jump down into my arms, I begged her. Quickly, jump before the old man looks out his window and sees us. She started to cry. Jump, I insisted. I'll catch you, and then she jumped. I can still remember the sound of my collarbone cracking when she landed on me.

I howled so loud the old man heard me and came running out of his house. He wasn't mad like we thought he'd be, just worried about the two of us. Sis was mad, though. She was the one who had to borrow money to pay the doctor.

How different my sister Mary is from my wife, Mary. Taking over when Mama died was an awfully big responsibility for Sis. I don't think I ever saw anyone work as hard as Sis did when we were growing up. She was always up and dressed an hour earlier than everyone else, making sure Agnes and I were ready for school, and that we had some porridge before we left. Right after school, she'd race home and do the housework and the cooking all by herself until Agnes and I were old enough to help. It was only when we were in bed that she started on her school work. It was amazing that she did as well in school as she did, considering how exhausted she must have been most of the time.

After spending most of her youth raising Agnes and me and looking after my two older brothers and Father, I expected that Sis wouldn't have any kids or maybe one at the most. Instead, she goes and has three. And still, her house is spotless. What a difference from my wife, who can't even keep the house clean with two kids. I can't remember when I've come home to find the sink empty of dishes. My wife says I should hire someone to help her once a week like other doctors' wives have.

I guess I never realized how much Sis gave up to keep our family going. I should make a point of seeing her more often. I don't give a damn what my wife thinks of her and Agnes. I'm going to have all of them and their kids over next Sunday for dinner, even if I have to cook it myself. If my wife's too good to grace us with her presence, piss on her. Nobody in my family will miss her.

I certainly don't miss her. That's for sure. In fact, it's great to be away from her for a few days. Still, I wonder why she hasn't called the office. She must know I'm here. Where else would I be? It's been three days now since she and that goddamn priest chased me out of my house. Maybe she's left me. No, she'd never leave me. She's probably just mad about the hospital thing. God only knows how embellished the story was when she heard it.

Thank God, the word hasn't filtered back to Agnes. She would be so upset I was suspended, and for drinking yet. Chances are pretty good she won't find out. My wife never calls her, and Agnes doesn't know any of the people at the hospital. I'm sure as hell not going to breathe a word.

Agnes asked me to stay for supper, but I said no. I'm not going to mooch any meals there when they don't have enough money for the phone. I offered to lend her some money, but she's too proud to take it. She's like me that way. Still, there's no need for pride where I'm concerned. We're too close for such nonsense.

When I left Agnes's house, I didn't have anywhere to go, so I went to Dugan's early. The place was almost empty. I had two small bags of pretzels for dinner. In my current frame of mind, I'd rather drink than eat.

By the time Driscoll and Bertie came in, I was loaded, but at least I was in better spirits. Talking to Patty always does me some good. It's too bad she's as plain as she is. She'd make some lucky man a great wife. Men are stupid for caring so much about a woman's looks. That was my downfall. Mary was so pretty before we got married, I didn't pay any attention to her rotten personality. Now, look at her. All that's left is her miserable disposition. If I'd been smarter, I would have found someone like Patty or Sis or Agnes instead.

Driscoll took over the gallbladder operation for me today. I appreciated that and bought him a couple of drinks to show him I meant it. Nothing interesting going on at the hospital. At least they have tired of gossiping about me.

MARCH 25, 1935

I had several patients this morning. Agnes's health has been preying on my mind, so I went over there and gave her a complete physical. I took a bottle of cough medicine for her. It's really strong stuff, but it will get all the phlegm out of her lungs and keep that hacking cough of hers down.

I noticed she had a bruise on her cheek. It took a while, but she finally admitted that Lee hit her during an argument. I was so angry I was ready to drag him out of the bar and knock the shit out of him. She begged me not to. Said it was her fault. At least his job is paying the rent, and she doesn't have to worry about that any longer. Still, I don't think their marriage is going very well. I'm not really surprised. Agnes has a stubborn streak in her. They argue quite a lot these days from what Sis told me.

Patricia came home from school while I was there. She has turned into a pretty little thing, with Agnes's big, brown eyes. But she's so quiet. She hardly said a word. What a shame to have a child's natural exuberance stifled by fear. It reminds me of how Agnes and I used to hide when Father came home drunk. The slightest little thing would set him off. We'd get the daylights beaten out of us if we caused any commotion. How quickly we learned not to make a sound when he was home. A cloud of sadness hangs over that house. It poisons the spirit of anyone who lives there.

I felt I had to get them out of there for a little while at least. The weather was so beautiful today it would have been a crime to waste it staying indoors. We got in my car and drove down to Rockefeller Park where the big beds of daffodils are in bloom. For an hour we just walked around the park, drinking in the sweet spring air. It did all of us some good. Helped us put our troubles behind us.

MARCH 26, 1935

I spent last evening at Dugan's again. Driscoll said the rumor was Mullens had suspended me for three weeks. I'm furious. I've got to do something. Three weeks is ridiculous. I have patients who are counting on me. I've already had a devil of a time getting Driscoll and Bertie to bend their schedules to take on some more of my cases. What the hell are my patients going to think if they hear I've been suspended? And for drinking. That kind of crap leaks out.

I suppose I'll have to do something soon before Mullens ruins my practice. What I'd like to do is take that little bastard and strangle him with his own intestines.

Still no word from my lovely wife today. She must be devising some wonderful torture for me. As much as I would love to call her bluff and force her to phone me, I need to get some clean clothes. I've already bought some underwear and shirts, but I can't keep wearing the same suit. I may have to break down and go over there tomorrow. I wish I knew of a time when she wouldn't be there so I could sneak in and get my clothes without having to talk to her.

I bought myself some franks and beans and a little pot to heat them on the hot plate that I use for coffee. Now I wish I'd stopped somewhere and had a real dinner. I haven't had any decent food in days.

I don't know what I'm going to do with myself this evening. I'm getting damn sick and tired of sitting around Dugan's. I guess I'll find another bar and somebody new to talk with, rather than go crazy staying here in this office.

MARCH 27, 1935

Maybe I shouldn't write when I'm so far into the bottle. People say I'm an entirely different person when I drink. That's a bald-faced lie! I'm an entirely different person when I'm sober.

When I'm sober, I'm what other people want me to be, not what I am. The real me stays all covered up. That's why I don't drink with people I don't like. They don't deserve to know the real me. At Dugan's it's just the opposite. I'm never anybody but me, no matter how much I drink. I'm not Mary's husband or Frankie's father or Martin's cousin. I'm just Frank. Good old, handsome, wonderful, generous Frank.

Patty says I'm funny when I drink, but I like to think my wit doesn't come out of a bottle. It's just that most people don't understand my kind of humor. It makes them uncomfortable. So, most of the time, I put a lid on my kidding, so people around me don't get pissed. Except at Dugan's, of course, where it doesn't make any difference.

I don't know why I'm going on like this. I should be worrying about where I go from here. I've really done myself in this time.

This afternoon, after I had fortified myself sufficiently, I went over to the hospital to talk with Mullens. To reason with Mullens. He didn't want to see me. He made that clear enough. I insisted ever so gently that he give me a few minutes. How goddamn humiliating for me to have to beg him for five minutes of his time.

I affected my most humble manner. I practiced it all the way over there. Sir, I called him. I can't believe I actually called that sheep's prick sir. I truly beg your pardon if anything I have done has offended your most elevated standards for this institution. I am sincerely apologetic and seek your forgiveness. What a sorry taste that speech left in my mouth, but I said it with a straight face. I'm not without theatrical ability.

Frank, he said, puffing himself up like a turkey in heat, it's my duty to maintain an elite cadre of highly disciplined physicians at this hospital. You have breached that and must be severely punished for it. You're suspended from surgical privileges for two months, starting today. I don't want to see you even near this hospital until I reinstate you.

I was floored. What am I going to tell my patients? Two months is outrageous, and I told him so, still trying very hard to maintain my composure. He waved me away like some lowly orderly and said he didn't have time to argue with the likes of me.

I couldn't stop myself. I grabbed the little sonofabitch, yanked him off the floor, and shook the daylights out of him. I don't even remember what I said. All that sticks in my mind is the terrified look on his face. I just wanted to kill him, and I'm sure he knew that.

I'm finished there.

MARCH 28, 1935

I went home last night and told Mary everything. I wanted her help in figuring out what I should do next. What a mistake that was. She had already talked to someone at the hospital, probably that carrot-topped cunt Helen.

She cried and yelled at me from the minute I walked through the door. She couldn't find it inside her to forgive me or even understand my side of the story. She just took it for granted I was wrong, and Mullens was right.

I think she's finally shown her true colors. She didn't marry me. She married a doctor. She bought a ticket to money and social standing, and now she feels cheated. She doesn't give a damn about how I feel and the crisis I'm having. All she cares about, all she ever cared about, is herself.

She said she's leaving me. Good riddance. I don't need a wife like her.

What an ugly sneer she had on her fat face. I was no good, she yelled, a crazy drunk, just like my father. Her friends had warned her, her lousy fat girlfriends, not to marry an Irishman. They're all drunks, they told her. God, how I hate her. I just wanted to strangle the life out of her.

If I was such a bastard, how come I spent every cent I made on things that made her happy? In a city where half the people don't have the money to buy a decent meal, she goes out and buys a set of new china dishes.

I went over to the cupboard and threw every one of those expensive dishes on the floor. From the look on her face, you would have thought I was bashing in the skulls of infants. If you're leaving me, I told her, you won't be needing these. And me, I never ever needed them.

I went upstairs and packed some clothes. The door to the boys' room was closed. I can't imagine they could have slept through all that racket, but at least they weren't crying. I wish now I had gone in and talked to them.

MARCH 29, 1935

I went to Dugan's last night. Maybe for the last time. The heads turned when I walked in. Bertie wasn't there. I wonder if he stayed away purposely, so he wouldn't have to see me. Driscoll was there, but then Driscoll's always there after work. He was friendly to me, but it wasn't the same. I have crossed over the line. He kept looking around at the other people from the hospital who were watching us. He's nervous about being seen with me. Even with all the money his family has, he still has to deal with Mullens.

Too bad it was Patty's night off. She would have given me a sympathetic ear. No reason for her to change colors on me. I had one drink and left. I was feeling really rotten. Having all those sanctimonious hypocrites from the hospital around me did nothing to lift my spirits.

I needed some excitement and loud music to take my mind off things, so I decided to go slumming and check out a few of the dives on Prospect that everybody talks about. Those people there surely don't give a damn if you roughed up somebody.

It's the dregs of humanity in those bars. Very absorbed with the basics. Like finding their next drink. Sex. Stealing a warm coat or a new pair of shoes. But they were having fun, and so was I, watching them. Poor as they were, they were laughing and dancing and shouting. It made Dugan's seem like a church social.

Just a few patients today. I slept off the ghastly hangover I had from my outing last night. There was nothing much to do all day except read the paper, listen to the radio, and drink.

Only one person called, my cousin Martin. He wants to meet me downtown for lunch tomorrow. I hope it doesn't mean Mullens is going to press charges. No, he couldn't do that. The hospital wouldn't expose itself to the publicity.

I wonder what would cause Martin to call me. He never calls me. The only time I ever see him these days is at weddings and funerals. I guess we've drifted apart over the past few years. He's busy with his work and me with mine. The whole family used to get together at least twice a year, once in the summer for a picnic in his backyard and then again at Christmas time. I'm not sure why that all stopped.

I've got to get out of here tonight. I can't stand to be cooped up in the office any longer. I guess I'll go back to Prospect Avenue again. At least nobody knows me there. I won't get any shit about what I did to Mullens.

MARCH 30, 1935

Another beautiful day in Cleveland. It's been pouring ever since this morning. I sent off two letters to local hospitals today to see if I could develop an affiliation with one of them. Beatrice, the lady in the office across the hall, was kind enough to type them for me. It's not going to be easy finding another hospital, particularly when they check on my reputation with that sonofabitch Mullens.

In the meantime, I need to get some more nonsurgical patients. I had Louie change the sign on my office door to say Physician instead of Surgeon. I can always change it back later. Things have been abnormally slow. Only had one patient today. I examined him and referred him to Driscoll for surgery.

I called up the hospital and told them to send my things to my office. Margaret was real nice. Said she was sorry I wasn't there anymore. That makes two of us. Goddamn Mullens. I hope he rots in hell.

I met Martin for lunch downtown at the City Grill. I must say he is doing well for himself. He looked real dapper in his camel hair coat and new gray suit, very much the image of a successful congressman. I tried to keep the conversation on politics, the subject he loved, but it didn't work. He got right to the point. He heard about Mullens and was concerned about the family and me.

He started in about Father. How his drinking had broken up the family. He said before Father started drinking so heavily, the two sides of the family had been very close. Every time there was a birthday, we'd go over to celebrate at Uncle Dominic's. Martin said the reason all that stopped was that Father started getting drunk every night. Dominic didn't want him in his house when he was drinking so heavily. So, the birthday parties ended, but we all still got together at Christmas until Dominic died. After that, we didn't get together much at all.

Then Martin started in about Mama and what Father had done to her. I hadn't really thought about it before, but Martin had known Mama much longer than I had. Martin was about eighteen when she died. He went on about how much she suffered and how the family blamed her death on Father. That's where I stopped him. I wasn't going to listen to anyone, not even Martin, say that Father had killed her. It just can't be true. Martin's just exaggerating, as usual.

It's strange what you can recall from your childhood and what things slip away forever. I remember as though it were yesterday, Sis's fit over the mitten that I lost when I was nine or ten years old, but I can hardly remember my mother's funeral. It must have been the saddest day of my life, but I absolutely cannot remember anything but the sketchiest details.

I told Martin I didn't appreciate him talking the way he did about Father. Yes, he drank too much, and sometimes he got violent, but then he was in a lot of pain because of his back. As much as I hated Father and despised what he did to us, I'm very sensitive about anyone, even my cousin, talking about him. Maybe it's because I'm so ashamed of what he was. I'd just as soon forget he ever existed.

Martin is so concerned I'll end up like Father, but I told him not to worry. I can stop drinking anytime I want to. Besides, compared to Father, I really don't drink that much at all. And I'm a doctor for Christ's sake. I'd know if things started to get out of hand.

Just then, a big red-faced man in a nice-looking suit came over to the table to see Martin. Martin introduced him as one of the municipal court judges. He sat down and joined us for coffee.

I was particularly relieved to have the subject of conversation shift from me to city politics. I just sat and listened. Most of their conversation was about what a nincompoop Mayor Davis is, but there was one piece of news that got my attention. Martin's friend had just heard a rumor from someone fairly high up in the government that Eliot Ness, the man who got Al Capone in Chicago, was coming to take a job with the IRS in Cleveland.

While Martin and his friend were talking, I excused myself and told Martin I had some patients to see. It wasn't true, but it was a plausible way of getting out of there.

Later, I went over to Agnes's where Lee was home for a change. Agnes was very somber, but Lee was real happy to see me. He grabbed my hand and shook it. Said he'd heard about how I punched out Mullens. How the story changes as it gets passed around. He congratulated me, wished he could do the same thing to his boss.

Agnes started to cry. Very softly. Lee didn't even notice. It looks like I'm everybody's big disappointment in life. I only stayed a few minutes.

MARCH 31, 1935

I went slumming again last night and stopped in The Squire. I hadn't been there in years. It looks like it's becoming a queer bar, of all things. Walter's still tending bar himself. Old bastard must be in his late sixties by now.

I asked Walter why he let all these queers in his bar. He said he didn't care as long as they left him alone. He told me his business was actually picking up now that the queers were coming in all the time to meet other queers.

I don't see how he can stand to be around them. It drives me crazy to listen to that way they talk. I think old Walter is making a big mistake letting his place get known as a queer bar. He'll never get his regular customers back, and eventually, those damn queers will flit off to some other bar and leave him with an empty place. I told him so, but he didn't listen. Germans are like that. They're so stubborn, like Pollacks.

There was a nice, clean-cut blond kid sitting by himself next to me at the bar. He couldn't have been more than eighteen or nineteen. He didn't look like one of the queers, so I struck up a conversation about how the Indians might do this season. He was from New York City and a big Yankees fan, but he said as long as he was here in Cleveland, he'd go to the Indians games. I bought him a beer, and he shared some of his pretzels with me. It wasn't a half bad conversation.

If my powers hadn't been under such a cloud last night, I would have seen the problem coming and avoided the whole mess. I was anxious to get out of there, so I downed my drink and headed to the back to relieve myself. A few minutes later, the blond kid came in the john and started combing his hair. I didn't pay much attention to him. But after I took a leak, he came over to me while I was washing my hands. Goddamn, if he didn't turn out to be one of Walter's queers trying to get friendly with me. I grabbed that cocksucker by the throat and pinned him to the wall. The next thing I knew, Walter was in there pulling me off the guy. Walter, I said, I don't care if you like these bastards, but if one of them ever puts a hand on me, I'll cut it off.

I'm not sure why I'm so touchy about queers. It probably goes back to the war when I was a medic. There was another medic I was real close friends with named Eli. I can't think of his last name anymore.

The friendships that built up during the war were particularly intense. Sharing the fear and horror with someone on a daily basis creates a real bond between men. And living day and night with the same person over so many months spawns a kind of natural intimacy.

Eli was an extraordinarily handsome man with black hair and huge, dark eyes. The nurses were crazy about him, but he didn't pay much attention to them. He was an intellectual, an English teacher by profession and a poet of sorts. We'd often spend our few hours of free time talking about the couple of books we were able to get our hands on. He was, to me, a small oasis of sanity in a world gone mad.

Then one day, it all fell apart. We were in the showers together, just the two of us. I looked over at his fine, slim, muscular body and wished I had a face and body like his. The next thing I knew, I had an erection. I was just overwhelmed with embarrassment.

I prayed he hadn't noticed, but he had. His eyes locked in contact with mine. His big, dark, searching eyes signaled to me his approval. He didn't say a word.

I was very shaken by that experience. The bond had been broken. I avoided him after that and worried a lot about myself. I remember the sadness in his eyes the few times we glanced at each other.

I was the one who found him a little over a week later, lying in the trenches with the side of his head blown off. Even today, so many years later, I am so upset when I think back on it. I'm not sure if it's the attraction I felt for him or my breaking off our friendship just before he died that makes me feel worse.

APRIL 1, 1935

I decided after last night, I'd stay away from The Squire for a few more years. I wasn't anxious for any more incidents with queers. I went back to the bars on Prospect where I had such a good time a few nights ago. Those places are much more educational. There is a phenomenon in these downtown bars that I didn't see much in the places I normally went. These creatures have developed a code of behavior and a kind of pecking order one would expect to see in a society of chimpanzees or orangutans.

The minute a man dressed in a decent suit walks into one of those bars, up go all the antennae of the little beasts inside. I suspect their first instinct is self-preservation. They need to figure out whether the man who came in is prey or a potential predator, like a plainclothes cop.

Then the pecking order comes into play. First are always the prostitutes. There are usually at least three or four of them in those bars. Naturally, these whores will range in age and attractiveness. Particularly interesting is that without any conference or signals among them, the whore most likely to succeed with a particular client is the one who makes the approach.

I've watched this process now about ten or twelve times, and a pattern emerges. If a relatively attractive or prosperous looking stranger comes into the bar, the youngest or best looking of the whores goes after him. Whereas, if the man is ugly or poorly dressed, it's the less attractive or older whores who approach him. If he isn't interested in the whore who approaches him, none of the other whores will go after him that night.

Thank God, they don't know I'm a doctor, or all I'd hear about are their gynecological problems, which must be considerable. There is an irony here. I'm a doctor looking to expand my medical practice, and these bars probably represent more medical problems per square foot than any other place in the city. But I can't imagine having these creatures as my patients even if they had enough money to pay.

The two-bit con men come after the whores in the pecking order. They are generally more interesting than the whores, although I must confess I'm disappointed by their lack of creativity. No wonder they're such losers; they set their sights so low. Most of them are looking to talk me into buying them a few drinks or giving them my spare change for a meal.

At least they offer some amusing conversation while they drink whatever I feel like buying them. Once or twice, they've tried to sell me a watch or a fake diamond ring. One jerk tried to get me to follow him out to the parking lot to see some stolen suits he said he had in his car. As though I would be stupid enough to do something like that.

Maybe I should have gone out with him. I could have beaten the slop out of him and any friend he had waiting out there. Still, I don't need any broken knuckles. It's hard to operate on a patient with your hand in a cast.

APRIL 2, 1935

Martin's comment the other day about Mama's death has really troubled me. I can't seem to get it out of my mind. I even dreamed about her last night. In the dream, I was a doctor instead of a child, sitting at her bedside, doing everything I could to make her well again. I was frantic, trying to save her, but she quietly slipped from me. I woke up soaked in sweat on the agonizingly uncomfortable couch in my waiting room.

I didn't have anything to do today, so I went over to the old neighborhood to see if Mildred Reilly still lived next door to our old house. I haven't been back there since we had to put Father in the hospital. Some hillbillies answered the door at Mildred's house. They never heard of her. I tried the house on the other side where

Porters lived, but they're gone too. And the same with the Langs. Everyone's gone.

As a last resort, I went over to Holy Name and looked up some of the nuns who had been there since Jesus was a kid. One of them said Mildred lived with Micki now, her oldest daughter, over in Garfield Heights. Svec's her married name. I remember when Micki and Joe were married. They had the reception at the veteran's hall. Nice guy.

I looked her up in the telephone book and called. Micki answered. I talked with her for a few minutes, and then I asked her if it would be okay to stop over. She was delighted, and so was Mildred, whose loud, hoarse voice boomed in the background.

When I got to Micki's house, it was clear that she had done well for herself in marrying Joe Svec. They live in a nice house right near Garfield Park. Joe's now a manager for the telephone company. Good, steady job. Micki has three daughters and is taking care of Mildred and her mother-in-law, who seems to be getting a little senile.

Mildred is looking well, though. She hasn't seemed to age much. The only thing is that her arthritis is getting quite bad and it's very hard for her to get around. But, she's still the same old Mildred. Barroom voice. Swearing like a sailor. Shanty Irish and proud of it. I've always liked her.

When I got to the house, Micki had lunch ready. Jesus, has she ever put on weight. She must be awful close to two hundred pounds. I remember when she used to have a terrific figure. She must be eating all those wonderful Bohemian pastries she fixes up for Joe. She put out a plate of them, and I ate every last one. I can't remember what she called them, but they have apricot and prune fillings. I could live on them.

After lunch, Micki went to the store and left me alone to talk with Mildred. I couldn't very well start questioning her about Mama's death, so I eased her into the conversation by telling her I wanted to know more about Mama. Since Mildred was her closest friend, I thought she might be able to help me.

Mildred nodded approvingly. Now Mildred loves the sound of her own voice and would talk to me until next March if I would listen. To Mildred, there are no simple, straightforward events. Everything must be understood in its rich complexity of circumstances. I knew I was in for at least an hour, maybe even longer, but what else did I have to do with my time? Micki had left a bottle of whiskey on the table for us. I poured a shot for Mildred and myself and let her start wherever she wanted to in her memories.

She asked me first what I knew about Mama's family. I told her it wasn't much. All I remember was that her maiden name was O'Mara and that she was born in Boston. When I told her I didn't ever recall meeting my grandparents or any of the O'Maras for that matter, she nodded sadly.

She told me my grandfather, Patrick Henry O'Mara, had been born in the west of Ireland. When he was a young man, his uncle invited him to come over from Ireland to join his construction company in Boston. The uncle didn't have any sons of his own and took my grandfather into his company as a junior partner. Over the years, the two of them made quite a success of the business, and my grandfather eventually took over the entire business when his uncle retired.

Mama and her older sister were raised in a great, big house in a fancy part of the city. Mildred said Mama showed her a picture, and it was every bit as grand as those big houses in Shaker Heights. They had servants too, a housekeeper, kitchen maid, and a part-time gardener.

I was surprised when I heard that. How could Mama have been born in those circumstances and end up the way she did in such poverty? I interrupted Mildred to ask, but she told me she'd get to that in due time.

She said Mama and her sister were sent to be educated at the Convent of the Sacred Heart in the mountains of western Massachusetts. The O'Maras had become very socially conscious and wanted their daughters to be educated properly so they could marry into important families.

That's what Mama's sister, Clare, did. She married a lawyer from a very wealthy family. Mama had shown Mildred a picture of Clare. Mildred said that Clare was a striking beauty with long hair and huge, dark eyes, but Mildred disliked Clare instantly. There was something smug and selfish about Clare that showed right through in the photograph. Mildred said Mama never said anything bad about her sister, but she knew Mama and her sister weren't close.

Clare didn't look anything like Mama. Mildred said from the picture, you wouldn't even guess they were related. Clare had a vibrant, self-confidence to her that so often goes with exceptional looks. Mama was pretty but in an entirely different way. She had a very quiet and fragile beauty like a delicate porcelain figurine.

Just as I was wondering how Father had gotten into her life, Mildred said when Mama was seventeen, she was home from the convent school during the summer. Father was a laborer in O'Mara's construction company. O'Mara used him to do some work on his house, along with some other bricklayers, and that's how they met.

Mildred was always very blunt about Father, even to his face. She absolutely hated him and still does with a passion down to this very day. Your father used to be a very handsome man, she said begrudgingly, before he got so fat and bloated from the drinking. Black, curly hair and dark, penetrating eyes. But he was a no good, cheating, lying seducer, she added quickly. The no good part I already appreciated, the lying seducer part was new.

According to Mildred, the trouble with these young, rich girls who were sent to a convent was they were never prepared for real life. They were too sheltered. Nobody ever warned them about men like Father. Consequently, they fell prey to a fair face and a scheming tongue. Mildred went on to talk about her own hard life as the second oldest of eleven children in a poor family. But, she said, at least she grew up knowing a lot about the world, especially men.

Mama told Mildred she loved Father the minute she set eyes on him. Mildred said Mama would have to have given him some encouragement for him to be so bold as to go after O'Mara's daughter under his own roof. She said Mama was so naive at the time that she didn't even fully grasp what he was doing when he seduced her. That's the goddamn nuns for you, although I didn't say that to Mildred. Mama told Mildred that Father used to wait until everyone was asleep and then he sneaked up the back stairs into her bedroom.

That is, until my grandfather got wind of it. From what Mildred said, Father, rotten sonofabitch that he was, went bragging to some of the other men who worked for O'Mara that he was screwing O'Mara's daughter. My grandfather hit the ceiling when he heard about it. He fired Father on the spot and told him he was a dead man if he ever showed his face around Mama again. That night, he had Father beaten up by some of his men. Serves him right. I would have done at least that, probably more.

A few weeks later, he left Boston because O'Mara fixed it so he couldn't get any more work in Boston as a bricklayer. He went to

Cleveland to stay with Uncle Dominic until he could get a job here. Mildred said he never even sent word to Mama to say goodbye.

My grandfather was so angry with Mama that he sent her back to the convent right away, but the damage had been done. She was already pregnant with John, but it was months before she understood the condition she was in. Mama told Mildred she was terrified of what O'Mara would do to Father when he found out, so she sold the little bit of jewelry she had and ran away from the convent. Somehow she found out Father had gone to Cleveland and came here in the dead of winter to find him.

Mildred was on the verge of tears as she told me what happened next. Poor Mama, alone and broke in a strange city. And when she found him, the miserable bastard didn't want to marry her. In fact, he had a new girlfriend. God, I wish he was still alive today. I swear I'd go knock his block off. How I hate him. At that point, I'd heard enough. I wished I'd just left well enough alone, but once I got Mildred wound up, I wasn't able to leave in the middle of her story. So, I stayed, feeling more depressed by the minute.

Mildred said it was then Uncle Dominic got involved. He told Father to marry her, or he'd break his neck. I can just imagine that scene. He had a reputation for having quite a temper. It's a damn shame Dominic didn't break his neck anyway. Of course, then I would have never been born.

After a very quick wedding, Mildred said they rented the house next to her. She said her heart just ached for Mama. It wasn't more than a month after they were married when Father started running around with other women and drinking up most of the money he made.

I asked Mildred why Mama suffered all those years without asking her family in Boston for help. Mildred said she wasn't sure, but she thought it was a combination of Mama's pride and shame over what she had done with her life.

As I thought about it, I realized there was something more that kept Mama with him. Something Mildred probably never saw. It wasn't always as bad as it seemed to people on the outside. Yes, there were many times, virtually every day for stretches of time, when he was a complete bastard. Drinking, swearing, beating us over nothing, but there were times he was very tender and loving to her and us kids too. I remember him every once and awhile pulling her down on his lap and kissing her passionately right in front of us. Then, he'd pick her up and carry her up to the bedroom and shut the door. It was hardly enough to offset his meanness, but it was something. Probably just enough to keep that spark of love alive in her.

I wasn't ready to sit through a couple of hours while she ran down every crime my father ever committed, so I pushed the story ahead the best I could and asked Mildred if she remembered the time a few weeks before Mama died. Mildred rolled her eyes up toward the ceiling and said she'd never forget if she lived to be a hundred.

Mildred said Mama never completely lost touch with the O'Maras. She wrote several times a year to a cousin on her mother's side. That was how Mama found out that her mother had died suddenly from pneumonia the winter after I was born. Mildred said one day, Mama got a telegram from the cousin saying my grandfather was desperately ill, dying from cancer. My grandfather wanted to be reconciled with his daughter and to see his grandchildren before he died.

Mildred said Mama came over to her house in tears. She wanted so much to go to Boston to see her father and show him the children, but Father forbid it. He still hated O'Mara and was glad he was dying.

Mildred convinced Mama it would be a sin to deny her father his last wish, so Mildred and Martin scraped up enough money for us all to take the train to Boston. There was the expectation Mama's family would give us the money to get back if indeed we ever did come back. None of us kids knew anything about it. Mildred had lent Mama a suitcase and helped her pack it secretly.

Then that night, Father, when he stumbled home stewed to the gills, found the suitcase and figured out what was going on. He flew into such a rage. Mildred said she could hear him next door even though all the doors and windows were closed.

My God, I remember that night too. I was sure he was going to kill her. He just kept punching and beating her. He stripped off her clothes and made her stand naked in front of us. Then he hit her with the leg of the kitchen chair he had just broken. When she fell to the floor, he turned on Sis. Sis was hysterical, crying, and yelling. He hit her so hard she fell back against the armchair and tipped it over. I ran with Agnes and tried to hide in the closet, but he came after us and beat us with the chair leg.

Mildred said her husband contacted Martin and the two of them restrained Father. They had to tie him to the chair to keep him down. Mildred said she threw a blanket around Mama and took her next door. Mildred took us and the suitcase over there too.

She said Mama was unconscious for hours. There was a big debate on whether to take her to the hospital. Martin didn't want to unless it was absolutely necessary because he was afraid the police would come after Father and put him in jail. Then he'd have a hell of a time finding work. Mama finally came around, but she couldn't get out of bed for almost a week.

Mildred said she'd offered to send a telegram to O'Mara and explain what happened, but Mama wouldn't let her. She was too ashamed. She still hoped that she would be able to go to Boston as soon as she could get up and around. But it was too late, Mildred told me. While Mama was bedridden, my grandfather had died.

Mildred told me Mama was never the same. She hardly ate anything and was too tired to get out of bed. Mildred said she tried to cheer her up, but nothing seemed to work. She kept getting weaker until she succumbed to the heart problem that finally killed her.

I have some dim memory of that time, probably just a bit before she died. Agnes and I had crawled into bed with her and held onto her. I think we sensed she was dying and tried to be as close as we could to her. Kids know things like that even when the adults won't tell them.

In the end, Mildred's story had quite an effect on both of us. I was sorry in a way to have dredged up such painful memories for the old lady. But, on the other hand, she was the only person still alive who knew the whole story. As sad as it was, it was a story that I needed to hear.

I thanked Mildred for telling me about Mama. To get her mind channeled back onto other things, I started her talking about her granddaughters, which cheered her up quite a bit.

Not so for me. The awful feeling of powerlessness I used to have when Father hurt her hit me full force. It's crazy to hate someone who's dead, but I do. I wonder what I would have done if Mildred had told me that story when he was still alive. Gone over to Cleveland State Hospital, pulled him out of the ward, and started punching him? He was so nuts in those last years, he wouldn't have even understood who I was or why I was hitting him. It wouldn't have been worth the trouble.

I've been doing a lot of thinking since I got back to the office. People can pretty much be broken down into persecutors and victims. I don't know if they start out that way at birth or whether different circumstances turn them into one or the other.

When I think about Mama and what I heard today, it seems to me that she was a born victim. She didn't have to have the life she did. She chose it. Even when it was so goddamn clear that marrying Father was the worst thing she could do, she stayed with him. I won't believe for a minute her parents wouldn't have taken her back. She just didn't try.

Mildred thought it was pride and shame that kept her from going back to Boston. I don't think so. I believe she accepted in her mind that she was a victim. As bizarre as it seems, she and Father needed each other. He needed to mistreat someone to make up for being such a loser and she, for some crazy reason, needed to punish herself for letting him get her pregnant.

Maybe in some abstract way, it doesn't make any difference. Martyrs need someone to martyr them. But what an effect it had on us. We were the unwilling victims of her weakness.

I suppose to some extent, we all recovered from it once we got out of that house, but not entirely. Agnes, particularly, troubles me. I see her on the same path that Mama followed. After what we lived through, she goes and marries a brute. Now little Patricia is a victim too. Where the hell does it end?

I guess it's had its effects on me too. I'm sure all those beatings I took as a child had something to do with my shyness. For years, I was afraid of people. To this day, I'm uncomfortable around strangers unless I've had a few drinks.

Lately, I've fallen back into the victim pattern myself. It's just a variation of Mama and Agnes. At home, I had Mary persecuting me, and at work, I had Mullens. No wonder I'm so unhappy.

APRIL 3, 1935

I'm getting day and night turned around. I don't really remember what I did after the bars closed. I think I went to an after hours place with some colored guy. I woke up this morning in a colored neighborhood lying in the back seat of my car. I'm lucky I still have my wallet. Not that there's much money in it these days.

I can't remember when I've ever had a worse goddamn hangover. I lay there in the back seat for what seemed like hours listening to the sound of the children going to school. I was too sick to lift my head off the seat. I didn't feel well enough to drive back to the office until late this morning, and even then, it was a real struggle. I threw myself down on the couch and slept until mid-afternoon.

I went over to the house today to see the boys. This separation is very hard on them, as it is on me. They don't understand why I'm not there with them anymore.

It's painful for me to see them so unhappy. They shouldn't have to be in the middle of this. I asked her if maybe we should try living together again. She sneered at that suggestion. Her mind was made up, and I damn well wasn't going to get down on my knees to change it. I went back in the living room and spent the next couple of hours playing with the boys.

I should just stay here in the office this evening. If I had any common sense, I wouldn't go out when I feel so rotten. I've still got almost half a bottle of whiskey which should hold me for the night.

No, I've got to get out of here. This office is driving me absolutely crazy. It keeps reminding me of what a goddamn failure I am. What could be lonelier than an office building at night? I am a prisoner of my own making.

My imagination has run wild. What had started as a small fantasy is growing into an obsession. I can't seem to put it out of my mind. It's almost like the one that I used to have during the war when I had all that anger bottled up inside me.

There was no emotional deliverance for me as a medic. No relief from the stench of decayed and burnt flesh. No refuge from the cries of the wounded and dying. No way for me to get retribution for the numbing horror that built up inside me until my mind almost snapped.

My only release was fantasy. I used to think of what I was going to do with a goddamn Kraut when I got my hands on one. Shooting wasn't nearly good enough. In my mind, I devised a slow and exacting punishment for everything I had seen and felt. I don't know how many times that fantasy went through my head. It seemed to keep me going during those awful war years. I never did it, though. The opportunity was never right.

APRIL 4, 1935

I tried out a new bar last night on Prospect called the Silver Bird. What a fancy name for a dump. The dirty walls are painted the most revolting shade of flamingo pink. In the back of the bar is a huge, hideous painting of what looks like a silver chicken on a black velvet background. And the smell in the place. It just reeks of onions and garlic.

The owner is a fat, stupid Cuban named Jorge. For some reason, he has taken a fancy to me. He wants me to bring in all my friends to his place. He thinks his bar is much too classy for the scum who come in there now. That's a laugh.

There's an air of violence in that place I felt as soon as I walked in. It made my skin tingle. With that mixture of spics, booze, and whores, I kept expecting any minute for someone to pull out a switchblade. Maybe I'm completely nuts, but it's the danger that attracts me to the place. It's so intense, right at the core of my most primitive passions.

The place was crawling with whores. There was one wildly voluptuous, dark-haired girl with miraculous breasts. I just wish I could be satisfied by something as simple as a quick fuck with a whore. It just wouldn't be enough, though.

Sometimes I think I'm losing my grip on reality. I can be sitting at the bar drinking, and then, gradually all the people around me fade into the background like I'm in some kind of dream. It's like I'm standing back and watching myself enact the fantasy. When it reaches its conclusion, and it's always the same conclusion, a tremendous feeling of pleasure sweeps over me with an intensity I have never felt before, like a long, extended orgasm.

APRIL 5, 1935

I better not go back to the Silver Bird anymore. I should have realized that these fantasies would eventually erupt into something physical.

That little, spic bastard will probably have his friends waiting for me. Except for my sore knuckles, I feel pretty good today. Beating the crap out of that punk released a lot of the tension that's been building up. What a stupid shit he was to pick a fight with someone my size, even if he did have a knife. But I'm glad he did. I haven't been in a real fight for so many years. I'd forgotten how damn good it felt to pound my fist into someone's face. Still, I can't damage these expert hands of mine because some spic pisses me off. I've got to get control of myself.

APRIL 6, 1935

I'm so restless. It's hard for me to sit still long enough to write. I can't get this damned fantasy out of my head. Even during the day, I relive it over and over. My mind keeps refining it, filling in more details. I find myself always on the alert for the chance to act it out. It will hound me until I do.

There was a whore who came into the Verdun last night. I noticed her as she worked the bar. She glanced at me but didn't come over to the booth since I was talking with two guys.

I watched her out of the corner of my eye until she left. She seemed to know a few of the people at the bar, but the two guys I had been sitting with had never seen her before. She must not come in there often.

I should have followed her. God damn me! It might be weeks before she comes back there again. I didn't realize how right she was. She's more than right. She's absolutely perfect.

The bartender at the Verdun said she only comes in every couple of weeks, and he didn't know anything about her. I sat for hours until one of the guys that spoke to her last night came in. He thought her name was Betty, and she usually worked the bars on Woodland and Kinsman around 55th. I left immediately and drove over to that area.

I didn't realize how many bars were around there. I spent the whole bloody evening trying to track her down. It's almost impossible to get any goddamn decent information out of those people if they don't know you.

So, there I sat drinking and dreaming. Bar after bar, but still no Betty or whatever the fuck her name is.

APRIL 8, 1935

I finally found her! I was sitting in Blake's on Woodland tonight when she walked in. This time, she wasn't going to get away from me. I moved my drink over to a table where I could watch her as she sat at the bar. I was so excited, I almost spilled my drink all over myself.

I caught her eye and smiled at her. She noticed me but kept on talking with some old guy at the bar. Every once and awhile she'd sneak a look at me. I'd always smile back when she did. I played the game. As excited as I was, I wasn't going to spoil everything by rushing her.

It was pleasant enough just to watch her for a while. She's quite slender with a very young face and almost childish features. Very small boned with that fragile quality I find so appealing.

Eventually, she came over to my table and sat with me. I hope she finds me attractive. Then I did something I know I damn well shouldn't have. I told her my first name and that I was a doctor. I wanted to impress on her I wasn't some run-of-the-mill guy in a suit. It seemed to work.

It was very difficult to sit there and chat with her when the desire inside me was becoming so strong. I almost couldn't control it.

After about fifteen minutes, she told me she had to leave. I almost pissed in my pants. I hoped she didn't see the panic on my face. I asked her if I could meet her later. She suggested that maybe we could get together tomorrow instead.

At last, I got my wits about me and told her to meet me at the Holder Tavern, which is close to my office. I said I'd wait for her there at eleven o'clock. She smiled as she left with the older guy at the bar.

As disappointed as I was that she left me tonight, I have some time now to plan everything for tomorrow. I'll buy her a couple of drinks at Holder's and then bring her back here to the office.

April 9, 1935

It's two-thirty in the morning. I'm too exhilarated to sleep. I'm at the pinnacle of my experience. Once again I am in control of myself. I know now the truth that has been hidden inside me for so long, the revelation I couldn't see before. Wouldn't see. I have emerged from the gray twilight of my repression. All the torment is behind me now. I have once and for all established my strength and my identity.

I must capture this entire experience in minute detail before my memory erases it. I may never be able to recreate the wild excitement I have felt tonight. It has taken me so many years of anguish to reach this peak, I want to savor it for the rest of my life.

I was so nervous when I went to Holder's, afraid she might stand me up, and all my anticipation would have been for nothing. I went early in case she came before eleven. I didn't want to miss her. She was, after all, a prostitute, and I couldn't chance her picking up some other man before I got there.

I sat there and worried. Maybe I should have suggested a place easier for her to get to. How would she get there anyway? She'd have to take a bus or have someone with a car drop her off. I cursed myself for my stupidity.

When eleven o'clock came and went, I knew she wouldn't come. It was my own fault. Why should she come all that way to meet me when she could find men so much closer. Had I really impressed her enough that she might look at me as something more than a client? Maybe someone who would keep her so she wouldn't have to work. God only knows how whores think.

I kept pouring whiskey into myself as the minutes went by. I had an eye on the door every minute in case she walked in. Fifteen past the hour and still no sign of her. At the rate I was drinking, I'd have been too drunk to do anything about it if she ever did come. I switched to beer.

At twenty-five past, all my fears were put to rest. I saw her long, dark hair as she passed by the window. I was beside myself with joy.

I waited until she came in and started to look around for me, then I stood up and waved to her from the back of the room.

She came toward me slowly. She knew she had a very sexy way of walking and did everything she could to accentuate it. Her coat was loosely thrown over her shoulders so as not to conceal the provocative sway of her sleek hips.

This sensuous advance was not lost on me. She must have seen that on my face as she drew closer. The long, straight brown hair hung down in her face, partially covering her left eye. I hid my nervousness with a broad smile. She winked back at me.

I took her coat off her shoulders and put it on one of the empty seats. Then I pulled out her chair and seated her opposite me. She was pleased with the courtesy I was showing her, something she was clearly unused to from other men.

I went up to the bar and brought us back a couple of drinks. She was very quiet, almost demure. I did most of the talking, about trivial things like the weather. Slowly, she started to open up. Not that she had anything of real value to say, just the kind of drivel one would expect from a prostitute. I could tell she was starting to feel comfortable with me, attracted to me. I could see it in her eyes as she spoke.

She crossed her legs and brushed my leg momentarily in passing. That sudden, unexpected touch of her flesh sent a thrill through me. I had to repeat it. After a few minutes, I moved my leg against hers, very tentatively at first. She didn't move away. I pressed my leg more firmly against hers, and she smiled.

She seemed to sense my shyness with women, a defect I've tried for years to hide behind courtly manners, and let me work up to things at my own pace.

I asked her if she had to be home at a particular time, not wanting a repeat of what had happened last night. She said the buses stopped running at twelve-thirty, and she would need a ride home. I assured her I would drive her wherever she wished.

When we finished our drinks, I offered to show her my office. I told her it was almost next door. She liked that idea, and so we left through the back door. It's closer to get there through the alley, I explained. All the offices were dark except for the hall lights.

I led her into my inner sanctum where I have my desk, my books, and the couch I've been sleeping on. I turned on the small lamp on the bookcase, which gave the whole room a kind of dusky glow.

I showed her all the unique things I had collected and displayed in my office. Trophies I had brought back from Europe after the war and the souvenirs from my trip to the Canadian Northwest.

I told her to make herself comfortable on the couch while I got some ice for our drinks. When I came back, she had slipped off her shoes and sat with her feet tucked under her.

I took off my jacket, and she watched me silently as I folded it neatly and placed it on the chair. Then she motioned me over to the couch and stood up in front of me. Without her high heels, I towered over her. She reached up and loosened my tie. Why don't you take this off, she said, office hours are over. Then she undid my cufflinks and put them on the lamp table while I rolled up my shirt sleeves.

I sat down next to her on the couch and put my arm around her. She drew even closer. I was in no rush, so I lighted cigarettes for both of us and picked up my drink.

I had it all rehearsed in my mind earlier that night. The exact words I was going to use to explain the unusual request I was going to make. I had to say it in such a way that she didn't get frightened and leave. I also had to make it clear to her if she went along with what I asked, she'd get much more money than she usually did.

I was very nervous. Under the best of circumstances, I'm awfully awkward with women, even women patients sometimes. The prospect of asking her to do something so out of the ordinary was paralyzing me. I felt I had to ease into it.

I polished off half my drink and then I started. I have this recurring fantasy, I told her. She smiled coyly and pressed her knee firmly against mine. Tell me about your fantasy, she purred, putting my hand on her leg, just above her knee. Whatever I was going to say next was lost in the intense distraction of my hand on her body.

Very slowly and gently, I moved my hand up her thigh. Her hips started to awaken to my touch, drawing my hand farther and farther up her leg until I had reached the fabric of her panties. As though unconsciously stopped by the cloth barrier, my hand moved back on her thigh.

Shall I take these off? she asked softly. My mouth went dry. I nodded and watched hypnotically as she stood before me. With a few flicks of her wrist, her skirt came sliding down to the floor. Next came her black silk panties.

So slender and childlike in the lamplight, she could easily have passed for a girl of sixteen. Do you want me to take off my blouse too? she asked, confident of what my answer would be.

I sat frozen in place. Yes, I answered hoarsely. Yes, take it off. She started to unbutton her blouse while my fingers played nervously with the button on the cushion. My mind was racing ahead of me. Things were going faster than I had planned. It had taken me so long to come that far, I couldn't lose control of it that quickly.

I had gone to so much trouble to plan this evening in the greatest detail. I didn't want it spoiled because this whore had some notion of doing things her own way. It had to unfold the way it did in my fantasy. Things had to happen in a very specific order, or it was no good at all.

Maybe she was tired or bored with me and wanted to get it over quickly so she could go home. Or worse yet, go out again while the bars are still open and find another client. Yes, I thought to myself. That's what she wants to do. Get this over with and go back to work. I had kidded myself into thinking she was genuinely attracted to me. Her smiles, her coy glances, that initial demureness. All of that was a whore's trick. How many hundreds of men before me had seen that performance?

She stood in front of me completely naked, assured that she had taken matters into her own hands. None of my slow courtship for her anymore. Let's get down to business is what she was really saying to me. Time is money.

I sat where I was and did nothing. Anger was rising quickly inside me. She waited for a few moments and then she sat next to me, one arm draped around my shoulder. Here was the seasoned whore, experienced in encouraging the shy. Don't be afraid, she said to me in a patronizing tone as though she were speaking to a nine-year-old boy. Her hand reached for the front of my pants.

Not yet, I said, pulling her hand away roughly. She retreated, startled by the abrupt change in my tone. I pushed her down on the couch and regained control. She was surprised but satisfied I was at least taking the situation in hand. I sat on the couch beside her and put my hand on her breast. I squeezed hard. She cried out in pain and tried to sit up, but I pinned her back with my other hand.

You want this to be over soon, don't you? I said to her, still squeezing her breast. I thrust my fingers up into her forcefully. She cried out again. This time, I put my other hand over her mouth and pushed my fingers in deeper and deeper.

This must be the moment whores have nightmares about. Those quiet, lonely men who appear so easy to manipulate but turn suddenly into violent, angry animals. I'm sure she fancied herself an expert on men. She had me pegged as the shy, polite type she could use over and over again and discard at her whim. Now she knew she had made a terrible mistake in judgment.

The more she struggled, the more excited I became. I rammed my fingers in harder. Her whole body rocked with the power of my thrusts. Her eyes bulged with fright, and I heard her moan pathetically. Her terror just intensified my frenzy. I bit her breast hard and watched the blood appear on her chest, and then I bit her all over her body. The blood was everywhere on her now. I put my face down in it and lapped it up like a hungry dog. I wanted to completely consume her.

I yanked her to her feet while she tried to fight me with the little strength she had left. Putting my hands around her neck, I choked her into unconsciousness. Then I carried her into the small surgery and laid her out on the table.

She was mine now. Completely and totally mine. No tricks. No deceit. I carefully pulled back her long, brown hair and stretched it down over the end of the table. She lay there so still. I tore off the rest of my clothes and got onto the table with her. In that one brilliant, flashing moment, I will never forget, I took her. My power has never been greater. It surged limitlessly. Her body throbbed and convulsed, yielding completely and unconsciously to me.

APRIL 10, 1935

It's six o'clock, and I've slept away the whole goddamn day. I barely had the energy to get dressed. I've got to find some way of dealing with her. I can't put it off any longer. She's got to be out of here tonight.

I'm so depressed, I can hardly think straight. She is oppressing me, mocking me. I can't even stand to look at her. It's hard for me to believe this pale, stiff wretched piece of cold meat gave me so much pleasure last night. She is more trouble now than she is worth.

What a fool I was to tell her as much as I did about myself. With my luck, she told all her whore friends she was going out with a doctor named Frank. The police will look particularly hard at me because my office is so close to Holder's Tavern. Worse, either of us could be remembered by the people in the tavern last night. More people could recall me asking about her in those bars on Woodland. Goddammit, I sure have been stupid about this.

My only hope is that the police aren't going to spend any time looking for a missing whore. Whores must disappear all the time. I'm sure I'm not the only man in this city to vent his feelings on a prostitute.

[Note: This is where this volume ends. It is not clear if there is a volume missing or whether the author suspended his writing until the beginning of this next volume.]

SEPTEMBER 19, 1935

This is such a goddamn ugly city. I hate it. When I look outside my window, all I see are squat old buildings blackened by the soot of the mills. Trash and garbage blowing all around the street. Broken beer bottles and overflowing garbage cans everywhere. Bums huddling in doorways begging for the price of a drink. Skinny, half-starved dogs barking at every passerby.

Cleveland is a city of losers. Pollacks and niggers and hillbillies. To them, success is a full-time job in some sweatshop. They work their stupid asses off just for enough money to pay the rent on some falling down shack. Failures, all of them. Fools and victims.

Early this afternoon, I went out for a walk. Bought myself a sandwich and walked a few blocks up 55th Street. Right off 55th is Kingsbury Run, the ugliest place in this ugliest of cities. On the floor of this filthy ravine are the tracks of the railroads going in and out of the city.

Kingsbury Run is now home to the thousands of hobos who have flooded into the city in the past few years, living in their little corrugated metal shacks, trying to stay warm with their little fires. They huddle together in their torn coats, drinking the sterno that will eventually destroy their kidneys and kill them. Human garbage is what they are.

Yet depressing as it is, this Kingsbury Run holds a scary fascination for me. I stood for almost an hour watching those pathetic, ragged creatures. This ugly ravine, on whose rim I stood so shakily this afternoon, is the ultimate degradation. The final graveyard of impossible dreams and unfulfilled expectations. They watched me too, the hobos did. They looked up from their fires and saw me standing there watching them. Do they realize what a short, fast fall it would be for me to tumble down there with them?

How I hate this city. It's a cancer. A disease grown monstrously out of control. Choking and killing off any hope of recovery and rejuvenation.

SEPTEMBER 20, 1935

I've done it again. I swore to myself that I wouldn't, but I just couldn't help it. I didn't even plan it until I saw him last night in a bar on Central.

He was a short, stocky fellow in his forties from out of town. He was down on his luck and drinking a lot. I got to talking with him and bought him a couple of drinks. Then after the bar closed, I brought him back to the office and gave him something to eat.

While he sat there in my surgery, eating the sandwich that I made for him, I thought about how I was going to do it.

This time, it was very different than with the whore. Now, I was sure of myself and knew precisely what I had to do, but I was impatient. He must have picked up on that because he kept watching me out of the corner of his eye.

From the moment, I spoke to him, the need began building in me. It's like a ravenous hunger that won't be satisfied. All my wits and senses are subordinate to it.

I couldn't contain myself any longer. I went over to the sink behind him and started to putter around with some of the dirty glasses. Still carrying on my part of the conversation, I pulled a knife from the drawer and put it under a towel near the sink. I glanced over at him to be sure he hadn't seen it.

Then I grabbed him from behind and choked him with my arm. He gasped and struggled, but I tightened my hold on his neck even more. When he became unconscious, I pulled him over to the sink and readied my knife.

How sweet is that moment of ultimate power? His soft white throat stretched out before my knife. The single deep, determined cut, and his life became mine.

It's like the thrill of the operating table. I am a primitive god surrounded by priests and priestesses, preparing for a sacred ceremony. The ritual proceeds as they lay out the naked creature before me like a sacrificial animal. I open its skin and hold in my hands its most precious possessions. As exciting as that power is, the expression of it is so often incomplete and unsatisfying. Some get well, others improve, just as often, they worsen and die, regardless of my skill. I have so little control over that.

But the power to take the life is totally mine. The result is so clean and complete. I feel whole again. Rejuvenated.

I have denied myself too long. When the need arose, I suppressed it, but it didn't go away, it grew. Now that I have given in, one isn't enough. I must have another.

I'll have to wait until tomorrow. Everything is closed now. Next time, I want someone special. A challenge. Not another godforsaken, drunken loser. Someone young and smart, like that cocky, young punk who tried to get me to write him a prescription for barbiturates. Yes, he's just what I'm looking for. He would be worth the risk. It's too bad it's so late. I'd love to get him over here tonight.

SEPTEMBER 21, 1935

I'm sorry now that I wasted the three cents to buy the newspaper. The whole thing is completely devoted to all the religious bullshit going on around Cardinal Hayes. The city has gone completely crazy. You would think that Jesus Christ himself had just dropped in for a drink. I can't for the life of me understand why everyone is so thrilled about old Cardinal Hayes coming to town.

It's all over the papers, the radio stations are broadcasting events minute by minute. Ten thousand poor slobs lined Euclid Avenue today just to get a glimpse of him. Although I find this hard to believe, they expect a hundred and fifty thousand people to show up for his midnight mass at the Stadium tonight. All this for some gaudily dressed Irish priest.

Well, I've had my own little celebration here tonight with that young punk I met last night. He came into the Shamrock a little after nine. I purposely sat at a table alone, motioned for him to come over, and asked him if he still wanted the barbiturates. His eyes lit up.

I told him he could have the hundred or so pills I had in my office and a prescription for a lot more, but he had to do some special favors for me. He understood exactly what I meant and winked. I told him that I was on my way out to the parking lot in back, and he was to meet me there in five minutes.

When we got to my office, I told him to undress, which he did, leaving only his socks on. He stood there naked while I stripped down to the waist. He's a remarkably handsome boy. Nice long, lean body. A good set of muscles. A more highly developed chest than I expected to see on someone that slender. Perhaps he lifts weights.

I went over to him and put my arms around his shoulders. I asked him if he would mind doing something a little bit different that would greatly add to my enjoyment. He didn't seem to find my request the least bit unusual, especially since I put three ten dollar bills in his hand.

I took the piece of rope that I bought this afternoon and tied his wrists together behind him. I told him we would go into the other room where we could be more comfortable and pointed him toward the closed door to the surgery just across the hall. I followed behind him.

I pushed the door of the surgery open, and he walked in. I came in right behind, shut the door quickly, and turned the lock. The dim glow from the lamp in my study across the hall was shut off now that the door to the surgery was closed. The room was completely dark.

He heard the click of the lock and spun around to face me. What are you doing? Turn on the lights, he yelled. I could smell the fear in him, hear it in his voice. My nerves tingled in anticipation. The animal realized it was trapped.

My hands moved rapidly to his throat. He struggled and rammed his knee up sharply into my groin. Damn, the shock and pain of it loosened my grip on him. He was free.

I turned on the light. He was already several feet away from me when he saw the body of the other one lying naked on the operating table. His eyes bulged with fright.

I lunged at him and brought him to the floor, knocking over the wooden stand next to him. Bottles and jars crashed, scattering broken glass in every direction.

I pinned him down with my weight, his hands still tied under his body. He struggled to throw me off him, kicking and wrenching his body against me.

I had my hands around his throat again. His head twisted and gyrated violently as he used the strong muscles in his neck to loosen my grip on him. I pressed my whole weight down into my hands and squeezed tighter around his throat. His thrashing became weaker and weaker. His eyes closed. He was unconscious.

I dragged him over to the sink and carefully positioned his neck over it. It's becoming a kind of a ritual now. I am very ceremonious and precise, like Cardinal Hayes preparing communion at the altar. One long, deep incision and an ocean of ecstasy sweeps over me. I am transfigured.

SEPTEMBER 22, 1935

I've had one of my more brilliant ideas today. I'm very excited about it. It came to me as I was thinking about what to do with their bodies.

It hit me like a flash of lightning. Instead of cutting them up and dumping them in the lake like I did with the whore, I'll put them somewhere they are sure to be found. Why hide the bodies when nobody can tie those two back to me?

The more I thought about it, the more I liked the idea. It would be the most outrageous thing I've ever done.

Two nude headless bodies. This city can't handle that. The newspapers will go wild, and the police will go absolutely nuts trying to figure out who did it. Everyone in the city will be scared to death to go out at night.

All because of me.

Now all I have to do is make sure that I don't get caught with the bodies. I think I have the details pretty clear in my head now. It's a fairly simple plan.

This is a Sunday night. Everything around here is closed up tight. I'll wait until around three in the morning when the streets are completely empty and carry them down to my car in blankets.

Then I'll drive over to Kingsbury Run and park the car at the top of that big hill. That's about as close as I can get the car to the ravine. It's the ideal spot because all the hobos are camped on the other side of the gully, across the railroad tracks.

The real trick will be carrying them down that steep hill in the dark without breaking my neck. I wish I knew of some way to get my car in closer to the ravine. No, I'm sure that's the only way it can be done.

When I get them down, I'll lay them out there, stiff and clean on the floor of the ravine.

I'm so excited, I've got goose bumps. I can't wait to see what happens when they find them.

SEPTEMBER 23, 1935

All day, I've been like a child waiting for Christmas. Several times I drove by Kingsbury Run, expecting to see police cars, but nothing happened until five-thirty this evening.

When they came, they came in droves. I counted seven police cars, not including the unmarked cars the detectives drove. I milled around in the huge crowd that was gathering, listening to their rumors and speculations.

There must have been thirty patrolmen and detectives combing through the trash and weeds. The police kept spectators more than a hundred feet away, so it was hard to see what was going on. Finally, the word spread through the crowd. They found the heads.

I wish I could be there when Coroner Pearse figures out that I stuffed the penis of the younger one in the older one's mouth and vice versa. I hope he gets a chuckle out of that.

I think he'll be very impressed this time. Even though the surgery is nowhere near as extensive as on the whore, it is quality work. Pearse has never tried to decapitate a human body with one single unbroken cut. If he had, he would understand how well you have to know your anatomy to do that properly.

Well, tonight is definitely celebration time. I'm going downtown and buying myself one hell of a fine dinner. I feel like a king.

THE JOURNALS:

CATCH ME IF YOU CAN

September 24, 1935

I cannot believe this. That goddamn cardinal took the whole front page and most of the first section of the paper. They put me on page thirteen. This city has its priorities all screwed up.

It was a pretty good-sized article, even though it wasn't on the first page. There was a picture of the younger one, Edward Andrassy. They identified him from his fingerprints.

The city should thank me for getting rid of that Andrassy trash. A cheap little hustler was what he was. Smoked marijuana. Broke up bars with his drunken fights. Sold dirty pictures. Pimped for the colored whores on Central. Prostituted himself. Jesus, I'm glad I washed my hands after I handled him.

The article said a few things that are beginning to trouble me. Some old bastard told the police he was walking his dog at the top of the ravine around three-thirty in the morning and saw a black Chevy sedan parked there. The papers didn't say anything more. Jesus, I hope that sonofabitch didn't look at my license plate. I wonder if he could tell it was a 1933 model. It could be a real problem if they start talking to everyone with a black '33 Chevy.

The other thing is that the article said one of Andrassy's friends was at the Shamrock Saturday night. Before Andrassy came out to the parking lot to meet me, he must have told his friend that he was going out with someone.

I hope the police aren't lucky enough to tie those two things together. Like the car and the guy in the Shamrock. Either of those things alone isn't enough to nail me, but both of them together would be a disaster.

SEPTEMBER 25, 1935

Not a goddamn thing in the newspapers today except my old friend the cardinal. He's having another one of his swell midnight masses again tonight. Doesn't the city ever get its fill of this shit? Maybe I'll go, just for a laugh. Wonder what he would do if he heard my confession?

Well, at least someone in the family made the paper today. There was a picture of my dear Cousin Martin with the cardinal at some dinner last night. I guess when you're an important politician you have to be wherever the cameras are. Still, it irritates me he's in the news when I should be.

I wish to hell I knew what was going on with that police investigation. I'd sure like to know if they're tracking down men with cars like mine. If I were a detective, I'd start with the owners of black Chevy cars who lived on the East Side. Then I would narrow that list to men who were strong enough to carry those bodies down into the ravine.

After that, I'd start to look at the alibis of the men on that list. Whoever didn't have a good alibi for that early Monday morning I'd put in front of some of the people who were at the Shamrock Saturday night, like Andrassy's friend and the two bartenders. See if anyone recognized the men on the list. That would be the logical way to go about it unless they end up with a list of three hundred strong men without alibis.

This is really worrying me. I feel like the noose is tightening around my neck. Of course, it wouldn't be hanging if they catch me. It would be the electric chair.

SEPTEMBER 26, 1935

Not a thing about the Kingsbury Run bodies in either paper today. The cardinal is still the main event. It's very hard for me to tell just what the police are doing when all I read about in the papers are those goddamn midnight masses. I need some more reliable sources of information.

I went to a place called Tony's Bar last night, right across from the Third Precinct Police Station. It's a plain, friendly bar with good food and decent whiskey. Tony, the owner, tends bar, and his wife serves up sandwiches and spaghetti. I sat for hours buying drinks for cops when they came off duty. It was most revealing.

Everybody knows everybody else there at Tony's, so it's not easy to break in on the conversations. I sat at the bar and ordered a drink. Then I started talking with the cop sitting next to me, making sure I told him early on that I was Martin's cousin. It made a difference.

A few minutes later, another cop, an older guy, came into the bar and started talking to the cop next to me. The cop introduced me as Martin's cousin. I made sure that I bought a round of drinks for the three of us, and we talked until the cop next to me went home.

That left me with the old timer, whose name is Dennis O'Donnell. Dennis is a short, little bit of a man in his early sixties with a head full of white hair. If he didn't slouch so much, he'd look a hell of a lot taller. Maybe that's what happens when you're a cop in a desk job for a number of years.

I bought us another round of drinks and asked him if he was working on the murders of the two guys in Kingsbury Run. He said no, that was for the detectives to worry about. There are four of them assigned to the case right now, but that wouldn't last unless there was a big break pretty soon.

I asked him if the two men in Kingsbury Run were connected to any other murders in Cleveland. He didn't think so. Fortunately, he told me, weird murders like that weren't very common.

Dennis told me the current theory was that one of the Bohemians or Slavs, of which there are so many in this neighborhood, caught these two guys fooling with his girlfriend and fixed them for good. These Eastern Europeans, he explained, learn how to butcher in the old country. It's second nature to them.

We drank for another hour or so, but I didn't learn anything more about the investigation. I had to be a bit careful about what I asked him, or I might draw too much attention to myself. What I need to do is meet more of the cops in Tony's, especially the detectives.

SEPTEMBER 27, 1935

There's still nothing in the newspapers about the police investigation. I'm not quite sure whether that's good or bad news for me. It seems like every reporter in town has been assigned to cover the cardinal's every move. I am more than a little annoyed that this faggot priest is taking up the whole damned newspaper when everyone in the city is wondering about the two bodies in Kingsbury Run.

The people in this neighborhood sure are concerned about it. I went to buy some cigarettes at the drugstore yesterday. The woman in front of me told the clerk she won't let her kids anywhere near Kingsbury Run until the police catch the killer. I get such a kick out of walking around listening to people talk about my work without realizing who I am.

I went back to Tony's last night and waited to see if Dennis would come in. He did, a little after six. I bought him a couple of drinks first and made some small talk, then I asked him how the

Kingsbury Run case was going. He said the detectives were getting nowhere on it and were ready to file it away.

I asked him if all murders were handled that way. They are now, he said, especially if the people killed are nobodies. It wasn't always like that, according to Dennis, but the police don't care anymore. They're out to feather their own nests.

Dennis said he was glad he was going to retire in a couple of years. He used to be proud to be a cop. A good respectable job. People looked up to you and trusted you. Now, it's completely different. The cops protect the crooks and make a lot of money doing it. It wasn't just the guys on the beat either. It went way up to the top of the department. In fact, he'd seen good cops turned down for promotion because the bad cops didn't trust them. He was disgusted. Didn't feel good about his job anymore. Just putting in his time until he got his pension.

I asked Dennis what he thought about this guy Burton who is running against Davis for mayor. From what I read, Burton's whole platform is cleaning up the corruption in the police department. Dennis said it doesn't matter. The mayor would have to fire half the police force to make any difference. It wasn't going to happen.

It looks like I don't have anything to worry about. The police don't seem to be taking this case very seriously. I wonder how many people you can kill before anyone takes any real action?

I stayed and bought drinks for Dennis until almost eight-thirty. Then I went downtown to look for some excitement, but it was pouring rain, and the whole damn town was closed up like a clam. So, I came back here, dried myself off, poured myself a glass of the good stuff, and picked up the newspaper.

DECEMBER 10, 1935

I hadn't been to Tony's in weeks. I stopped there tonight to have a few drinks with Dennis and his friend, a Plain Dealer reporter named Bill Hanley. Hanley is a tall, thin, hollow-cheeked creature with thick, horn-rimmed glasses perched atop his hawk-like nose. He's as homely as a monkey's hind end, but he drinks like an Irishman and holds his liquor almost as well. He christened my dead whore the Lady of the Lake when parts of her washed ashore.

Hanley was Tony's conduit for what was going on at City Hall. His aunt was a secretary there and got all the dope way before anybody else. Burton, the new mayor, was making sweeping changes in the whole administration, and Hanley had the inside track.

There were about ten of us hovering around the table with Hanley in the middle. He had a certain knack for dramatics and wanted to play his audience the best he could. He started out with the smaller stuff first, like who was going to be in charge of the port authority.

He saved the biggest scoop for last. The appointment that would affect nearly everyone in the bar. After an agonizingly long build up, Hanley said that Burton had called a press conference for tomorrow afternoon to announce the new safety director. He made them try to guess who it was, but nobody could.

Finally, he told us it was Eliot Ness.

It looks like Martin's friend was right last year when he said that Ness was going to capitalize on his fame in Chicago to get an important political position. With Prohibition over, it was silly to waste his talents hunting down two-bit moonshiners.

Hanley was really excited about Ness taking over the police force. If anyone could shake things up, Ness was the one. Dennis was skeptical. From where Dennis stood, the force was beyond repair. It took fifteen years of neglect to make it this bad, and it would take another fifteen years to make it better.

Dennis conceded that Ness might be able to get the recovery process going, but nobody, not even the guy who got Al Capone, was going to fix it overnight. Dennis didn't see Ness as the kind of man who would stay in the job long enough. He'd do a lot of flashy things like he did in Chicago and then dance off to his next promotion.

I had to side with Dennis. From what I had read about him, Ness looked like a guy on the move. For such a young man, he'd made quite a reputation for himself. He wasn't going to stand still in the safety director's position any longer than necessary.

Hanley agreed that Ness wasn't going to retire from the safety director's office in a place like Cleveland, but even if Ness were only in the position a couple of years, he'd throw off enough sparks to light up the whole city during that time.

After all, as Hanley said, Ness had only been in Cleveland since August, and he had shut down the largest bootleg liquor operation in northern Ohio. His agents were supposedly closing down a still every day. One of his raids caught two deputy sheriffs.

Dennis was starting to perk up as we talked about Eliot Ness. I think Dennis is really excited about the new safety director, but he doesn't want to get his hopes up too much. I understand how he feels. For almost nine months now, I've gotten my hopes up over and over again that some hospital would let me practice surgery there, only to have those hopes dashed by one thing or another.

I am fascinated by this Eliot Ness. I wonder what he's really like. Martin should be able to get me into the press conference Ness is having tomorrow.

DECEMBER 11, 1935

Today, I saw the new safety director. I sneaked into the press conference with my cousin. Martin disliked him instantly because Ness is such a Republican and Martin is such a Democrat, but I don't give a shit about things like that. I was very impressed with him.

It's not that Ness is dynamic looking. They say he's thirty-three, but he could easily pass for twenty-three. A real baby face, except for those eyes of his. They're so serious and determined.

He's very much at home with the newspaper people. Not even a little bit nervous. I didn't expect to see that kind of self-confidence in someone his age. He's a good dresser too. Expensive suit. Conservative tie. He looks more like a young stockbroker than a cop.

He's a lot taller than I had imagined. Somehow I had pictured him as this short, wiry little tough guy. Actually, he's almost my height. Slender. Very polished and urbane, much more so than the new mayor.

He told the reporters he was going to be as cautious as possible until he did his homework on what was going on in the police department. Although he didn't know what exactly he'd do yet, when he did, he'd take action first and talk about it later.

Martin says the politicians are getting real nervous about Eliot Ness. He doesn't care whose toes he steps on to build his reputation. The politicians are scared that the new brooms are going to find a whole lot of shit that's collected in the corners of City Hall.

I can see why Martin doesn't like him. It's much more than Ness being a Republican. Even though Ness came out of the same poor immigrant background that we all did, he's a real climber. He's using his brains to get himself ahead, whereas Martin has never tried to rise above his class.

I was surprised when Martin told me that Ness has a reputation for drinking and partying. How could someone have put their life on the line every day to close up the liquor operations in Chicago and still be fond of the bottle himself? He has to be motivated by ego, not thirst.

DECEMBER 12, 1935

I don't know why I'm as excited as I am over this new celebrity. Maybe it's because I'm so bored. I wonder what would have happened if Eliot Ness had been in charge back in September. I'll bet those detectives would still be burning the midnight oil in the Kingsbury Run case instead of dropping the whole thing in two weeks' time.

The Plain Dealer had several pages on him this morning. I didn't realize he had a master's degree in criminology. He's considered to be one of the best of the new scientific policemen, personally trained by the country's leading experts in police procedures.

I wonder if any of that learning will rub off on the morons who looked at my work as the work of a butcher. A butcher of all things. If those cops weren't so stupid, I'd be insulted.

DECEMBER 13, 1935

I stopped off at Tony's around nine this evening. Dennis was sitting with Hanley and another cop named Jack, who just got transferred into the Third Precinct from the West Side. Jack is a pleasant guy in his twenties. I'll bet my life he was a football star in school. Big, husky shoulders and a barrel chest. Dennis keeps razzing him because he went to college for a couple of years. That probably means a lot more to a cop's career now that Eliot Ness is in charge.

Jack told us about Ness's midnight tour of the Third Precinct. It started out with Ness hearing some sirens while he was having dinner with his wife at some fancy restaurant downtown. He sent his wife home in a taxi and ran out in the middle of the meal, following the sirens down a few blocks. The police were going after a burglar. Ness, dressed in his suit and tie, joined in the chase and was jumping over rooftops with the cops as they pursued the guy.

The burglar got away, but, from what Jack said, Ness was all invigorated by the chase. He had the patrolmen take him back to the Third Precinct station where he decided to go out on calls with Jack and his partner.

Jack said Ness was hell-bent to make a bust that night. It was a Thursday night, and things were pretty slow, so Jack and his partner, wanting to make a good impression on the big boss, took him over to one of the biggest whorehouses in the city. They called for some help and raided the place. Ness was real happy and went home after that.

Jack never heard of a safety director that went out on a bust with his men. Even the chief of police didn't do that. Chiefs and directors sat in their offices and were dusted off for important dinners or funerals.

Dennis, as usual, was still playing the skeptic. He didn't see a raid on a whorehouse as much of an accomplishment. More like a publicity stunt.

I had been quiet up till then. I said that it didn't matter whether raiding a whorehouse was small potatoes. Ness showed his men he means business. He'll roll up his sleeves with the guys in the trenches. The word will spread throughout the whole force very quickly.

From all our previous conversations, we all knew that Ness had three big problems with the police. Corruption, incompetence, and very low morale. Last night, Ness was working on the morale problem.

Hanley reminded us that Ness had worked with the most corrupt police force in the country when he was in Chicago. If anyone could smell a bad cop, Ness could. The difference, this time, was that the cops worked for him now. In Chicago, they didn't.

DECEMBER 14, 1935

These are the times that I wish I had gotten into a more exciting line of work. Maybe even a detective or an army officer. The trouble is that even with a college degree, those exciting jobs don't pay very well. Nothing like what you can make as a doctor if you're willing to put in the time. It's definitely a tradeoff between excitement and money.

General practice is boring the shit out of me. There's absolutely no challenge to it. Colds, measles, bronchitis. Crotch rot. Athlete's foot. I feel like an actor with a string of bit parts in bad movies.

Not so with surgery. Surgery is a starring role in a major production. All the lights and equipment and technicians. The thrill of the incision. The awesome drama of working inside a pulsating, living body. The constant danger that something may go wrong and precipitate a life-and-death crisis.

How I miss it all.

DECEMBER 23, 1935

I can keep my finger on the pulse of things at Tony's. The whole place was buzzing with Ness's surprise shakeup of the department that he announced late this afternoon.

Hanley gave me the details. It was just the two of us drinking tonight. Dennis had been dragged off Christmas shopping by his wife, and Jack had taken his girlfriend to dinner to celebrate his promotion to detective. Hanley called it the biggest police department reorganization in more than a decade.

A hundred and twenty some cops were transferred, promoted, and demoted. Hanley hadn't seen the whole list yet of the people affected, but the few names he did hear made it clear to him Ness had done a lot of homework in a very short period of time.

Hanley guessed that a good twenty to twenty-five percent of the force was involved in some kind of illegal stuff. Mostly bribery, but a few of them even did some of the mob's dirty work. No wonder the mob is so strong here.

After working as a police reporter for almost ten years, he saw the real problem as incompetence and low morale. The cops didn't care anymore. The few who did, usually the rookies, were so badly trained and equipped they were ineffective. Only made the morale problem worse.

Hanley and I stayed and drank ourselves into oblivion. I asked him if he had a family waiting for him at home. He said no, he was a bachelor. I teased him about it, and then I wished I'd kept my big mouth shut.

He told me he was engaged when he was a lot younger, but she died of some heart problem. After she died, he never had an interest in going out with anyone else. The way he said it almost brought tears to my eyes. Is it better to lose your love from an early death or watch it die by inches in a progressively miserable marriage? I think it's the former.

JANUARY 10, 1936

What a night. I'm really tired. My fingers are still so cold I can hardly write. I'm going to have to start carrying some warmer gloves with me if I do anymore chasing around with Hanley.

We were all sitting in Tony's around ten o'clock this evening when a cop came in and told Hanley that Cullitan, the county prosecutor, and Eliot Ness were going to raid the Harvard Club, the biggest gambling joint in the state.

We weren't going to miss this for the world. Jack, Dennis, Hanley, and I jumped in my car since I had a full tank of gas and a heater that worked. We raced over to the Harvard Club in Newburgh Heights.

When we got there, it was only Cullitan and about fifteen men waiting outside. Hanley said they were waiting for Ness before they stormed the place. Cullitan had tried to get in there with a warrant, but the owner, some slimy little thug named Patton, met him with a bunch of guys holding machine guns. He'd open fire on anyone who tried to get in, police or not.

Ten minutes later I started to hear the sirens. Soon, the sound was deafening. In no time, there were another twenty-five cars and almost as many motorcycles. It was like an invasion. In the first car was Eliot Ness, who jumped out before the car stopped and ran over to Cullitan.

Ness and Cullitan talked for a few minutes, and then Ness went up to the door of the club, completely unarmed, and pounded on it. Ness had the place surrounded by a hundred armed cops. Nothing happened. The door didn't open even a crack.

Ness picked several of the biggest guys, and they broke down the heavy door. I was holding my breath, waiting for the machine gun fire to cut Ness and his guys to pieces, but there wasn't a sound. Once the door came down, Ness and the cops stampeded the place. Not one goddamn shot fired. I couldn't believe it.

A few minutes later, they started bringing them out, customers and employees alike, with their hands in the air. Pretty soon they had all the cars loaded up. The photographers were having a field day. Everybody seemed to have one eye on the door, waiting for Ness to come out. Hanley and I were right near the door when Ness came out with Patton in handcuffs walking in front of him. What a mean looking sonofabitch Patton is. Patton said something to Ness that he didn't like, and Ness rammed him in the back with one of the confiscated guns, nearly knocking him down the steps. Patton turned around in a flash and raised his handcuffed arms to strike at Ness. It was wonderful. Ness had him down to the ground before Patton could even swing. The photographers went wild.

Afterward, we went back to Tony's where I dropped off Hanley in the parking lot. He had a lot of writing to do for the morning edition. Jack and Dennis went back to the bar to tell all their buddies, but I came back here to get some whiskey. I'd had enough excitement for one night.

I have to give it to Eliot Ness for having the guts to go after the mob the way he does. I'll bet they're planning his funeral as I write. I'm surprised he ever got out of Chicago alive. They say he's a crack shot, but he never carries a gun. Hard to believe.

All this excitement makes me restless. I guess I'm envious of this man and the recognition he gets. Tomorrow the papers will be filled with pictures of him and his raid. I will be reading the news instead of making it. Nobody takes me seriously.

JANUARY 24, 1936

I've decided to try my luck with whores again. There's less risk in it for me. They haven't got a chance of getting away from me like that Andrassy punk almost did. I need to be much more careful now that we have this shiny new safety director and his new homicide chief.

I went to a new place tonight on Carnegie. I don't even remember the name of it. It was a crummy bar filled with the steel mill crowd. It was too damned cold to go hopping from bar to bar, so I stayed there, even though I didn't like the place at all.

I think it's the class of people there I disliked the most. It's the swaggering, loud-mouthed blue-collar types who offend me. Everyone drinking up their week's pay. Swilling their beer, popping their shots, belching loudly. They're disgusting. The kind of place I'd expect to find Martin the night before an election.

It's funny. I don't mind the really poor people or even the cheap hustlers in the bars on Prospect. They're quite interesting in their own way. It's the lower middle class that's so tiresome.

The only good things about this bar were that it was very warm inside, and the whiskey was relatively cheap. The only practical problem was that I didn't see any whores. The few women there seemed attached to specific men.

I was getting ready to go back out in the cold and find another bar when she came up the stairs from the pool tables in the basement. She was short and plump with dyed reddish-brown hair. Her fortieth birthday had come and gone and taken with it any traces of good looks. After looking around the bar carefully, she headed right for me. She told me her name was Flo and asked me if I was lonely. I told her to sit down at my table.

Her round face had the coarse, hardened look of a woman who had been whoring all her life, but what she lacked in looks, she made up for in self-confidence. Right after she sat down, she told me that for five dollars, she would keep me warm and happy the whole night.

I couldn't help myself. I laughed and told her that I could stay warm and happy all night with a buck-fifty bottle of whiskey. After a little good-natured haggling, we agreed on two dollars. I can be very generous when I know I'm not going to have to pay out.

I told her I'd get my car and pull it up to the corner of Carnegie, which was a few doors down from the bar. That way, she wouldn't have to get cold walking with me all the way to my car, and I thought to myself, no one would see us walking out together.

When she got into the car, I saw she had a May Company bag with her. I asked her what she bought, and she pulled out a large doll. She collected them and had nearly seventy of them back in her room. She chattered like a magpie about her dolls all the way back to my office, as though I could ever be interested in such a thing.

Once I got her back to the office, I wanted to get right to the main event. There was no possibility of any exciting foreplay with this woman, not like with the other whore. I didn't even have her take off her clothes. I just showed her around the place and ended the tour in the surgery.

Things went very smoothly. I have mastered this whole technique, almost to the point of routine. Maybe that's the problem. I'm not getting quite the same enjoyment I used to. I still feel a wonderful sense of release, but the thrill isn't there anymore. I think it's because I'm rushing things too much. That night with the first whore was exquisite, the excitement of the hunt and the capture. I didn't realize how much that added to the total experience.

I was bored with this fat beast almost immediately afterward. I wished then I had made her undress first. Her clothes were just soaked with blood. I struggled to pull them off and ended up having to cut them off her. What a mess.

I should get rid of her tonight. Every day she stays here is an extra risk. If I don't get her out of here tonight, I'll have to stay here in the office all day tomorrow just to make sure Louie doesn't wander in here to see that the pipes haven't frozen over.

I'm just so tired, and it's so bloody cold outside. I still haven't thought about exactly what to do with her. I'll just clean her up tonight and worry about the rest of it tomorrow.

JANUARY 25, 1936

I didn't sleep well last night. I dreamed that Martin and Eliot Ness and about a thousand cops caught me and hung me from the top of the Terminal Tower. It was a silly dream, but it reminds me of how careful I need to be when I get rid of Flo's body. I'm sure as hell not going to risk going back to Kingsbury Run this time.

Just to make things easier for Coroner Pearse to recognize my work, I cut Flo's body in two pieces, just at the waist, the same way I did with the other whore. I didn't waste my time doing the careful surgery I did before. Any dumb asses who can't tell the work of a surgeon from the work of a butcher don't deserve any more of my time than is necessary to do the job.

In fact, I think I'll make my own little comment on that and put her body outside a butcher shop somewhere. The head's got to go somewhere they won't ever find it. Maybe in one of those big trash barrels they have outside the mills. I don't want to take the chance that someone will identify her and tie her back to me.

JANUARY 26, 1936

I slept late this morning. I was so tired from being out until three in the morning getting rid of Flo. After I wrapped her up in newspaper and put her in four large burlap bags, I drove back toward town until I found a butcher shop around 20th and Central. Parked my car a couple of blocks away and carried two of the sacks into the alley behind the butcher shop. Goddamn, it was cold. The wind just went right through my coat. Fortunately, with that kind of cold, there's no one outside to see me.

Just as I was putting the burlap sacks in a basket at the back of the shop, I heard a rustling sound. I turned around to look, but I couldn't see anything in the dark. I put the one bag deep in the basket, and then, I heard the sound again. This time, it was louder. There was someone there with me. I didn't know what to do. Should I drop the other bag and run, or should I pick up the bag from the basket and run with both of the bags? All of a sudden, I heard the most blood-curdling howl I ever heard in my life. I nearly jumped out of my skin. I whirled around and saw it less than ten feet away from me. An enormous dog.

It was up on its huge hind legs ready to lunge at me. I drew back and braced myself, still clutching one of the burlap bags in front of me. Then I saw the chain. It couldn't reach me. The dog started to howl again. I've never heard a dog so loud.

I dumped the other bag in the basket and ran like hell until I reached the street. I had to get out of there before the damned dog woke up the whole neighborhood. That really makes me mad. What the hell kind of degenerate would leave a dog out like that in sub-zero weather? The owners ought to be locked up.

I was going to leave the other sacks behind the butcher shop too, but I couldn't risk going back there and running into the dog's goddamn owner. I drove my car down a few blocks and put the other sacks in a garbage can behind an old boarded-up house.

Today, I'm just going to sit and wait. I'll keep the radio on in case there's something on the news. If it weren't Sunday, I'd go over to Tony's. Tony refused to pay the bribe for a Sunday beer license.

Of course, they may not find her today. The butcher shop is closed. In fact, they may not find her at all unless that dog gets loose.

As I was cleaning up my waiting room, I came across the doll. I took it out of the bag and looked at it again. It was a nice doll with a pretty child's face and well-made clothing. It looked expensive to me.

I wonder what a tired, tough old whore was doing with a doll like that, with a collection of dolls like that. What pathetic purpose did these idealized creatures have in her empty life? Maybe they were children she never had. Did they make up for a childhood she hadn't experienced? Perhaps all they represented was the timeless existence of pretty faces, clean clothes, and eternal youth.

I should have thrown out the doll with the rest of her things, but I didn't. I don't quite understand why, but I propped it up on my bookcase next to the picture of my boys.

JANUARY 27, 1936

I did it! I finally made the front page just like Eliot Ness. A big article right up near the top with two big pictures. One of the pictures was of the dog. I'll be goddamned if that dog didn't lead some colored woman to the burlap bags. The other picture was of some guy named David Cowles who the paper headlined as "Torso Investigator." Not a very attractive sounding title. If I were Cowles, I'd complain about that.

The colored woman went over to the baskets to see what the dog was barking at and thought she saw some hams inside. How unflattering for Flo, overweight that she was. The woman asked the butcher about the hams, and he went to take a look. That's when he found Flo's arm and called the police. Quite an impressive array of detectives this time, including our new Captain Hogan. There were six of them mentioned in the article, including this Cowles guy. Why on earth would they have a ballistics expert there? I never used a gun. Whatever respect I might have had once for Coroner Pearse went down the drain today.

First of all, he estimated Flo's age at between thirty and thirty-five. He's probably only off by a decade. The other thing he said is that she was cut up by someone inexperienced. That really pisses me off. I may have been hasty on some of the cuts, but the decapitation was superior. Pearse said nothing about the similarities between Flo and the Lady of the Lake or the Kingsbury Run bodies. It's inconceivable that they haven't connected them by now. After all, how many decapitated bodies do they find in any one-year period anyway? I didn't have any patients this afternoon, so I went downtown.

I stopped at the May Company and went up to their toy department to look for something to give to the boys. I can only guess what boys that age would like. I finally found a couple of trucks, a drum, and a toy doctor's kit. While I was there, I looked at the dolls. I never realized how many different kinds there were. There were some very nice dresses that should fit the doll Flo bought, so I bought a pink lacy one and a little rose-colored coat. I suppose at some point I ought to give that doll to Patricia, but right now I like it where it is in my office. It has a calming effect on me.

JANUARY 28, 1936

Sic transit gloria. There's nothing at all about Flo in the Plain Dealer this morning, but there was a big article in the Press last evening. By yesterday afternoon, the cops had figured out who she was from her fingerprints. She'd been arrested several times for prostitution. That's a problem with whores, they tend to have their fingerprints on file. I would have preferred that she'd never been identified. It's much safer for me, and so much less humiliating for

Flo. All those nasty details about her life being publicized. Who her scummy boyfriends were, how many bar fights she got into, who beat her up last week. I felt sorry for her having her life dissected so publicly. Last night at the bar, Hanley said the whole investigation focused on who was with Flo the day she died. They found a lot of people who knew her, but so far none of them would admit to seeing her on Friday. Dennis said they've got six detectives working on the case right now. All of them are working their asses off trying to impress Hogan, their new boss. I asked Dennis if this Hogan was any good. Dennis says he's been on the force for decades. A good cop with a reputation for being fair, but nothing special. Hanley says Hogan's not the smartest guy in the world, and he's stubborn as hell. He was promoted because he's honest and obedient. Like a pet bulldog, I gathered.

JANUARY 29, 1936

I found out when I stopped at Tony's for lunch why this ballistics expert Cowles was in on the investigation. He's one of Ness's right-hand men. Hanley said Cowles was one of the smartest guys in the department. He's completely self-educated and knows more about police science than any fifty men on the force. I like that. Ness has put his top guy on the project since it appears like there's no contest between Captain Hogan and me.

Hanley said something that's bothering me. One of the men who were at the bar where I met Flo told the police he saw Flo talking to a man before she left that night. He told the cops he could describe the man in some detail. He said he noticed the man especially because he seemed so out of place in the bar. Too well dressed to be in that place.

Swell. I knew I should have left that bar as soon as I saw what kind of joint it was. I had a bad feeling about it from the beginning.

Hanley said he was going out there this afternoon with the police artist they were sending to help recreate the face the guy remembers.

I wonder which one of those bastards it was. I didn't talk to anybody except the bartender when I bought my drinks. Come to think of it now, one of the guys sitting at the bar stared at me every time I went up for another whiskey.

Shit. I hope that sonofabitch's memory isn't any good. All I need is a good sketch of me published in the newspapers. Someone might even remember me talking to Andrassy and the other guy from back in September.

After I left Tony's, I went to the address the papers gave for Flo. It was a shabby rooming house on Carnegie. I told her landlady that I was a reporter for the South End News. She was very nice to me and invited me in for coffee. Then she took me up to see Flo's room.

Even though I knew Flo collected dolls, I was in no way prepared for what I saw when I walked in. There were so very many dolls in that one small room. They were everywhere, on the floor, on the bed and chairs, and even hanging in little baskets from the ceiling.

It was a very strange experience for me, being in her room like that. Almost as though I could feel her presence there, like she was still alive somehow in that artificial fairyland. In a way, I wish she were still alive. I liked her sense of humor.

I went over to the table near the window and looked at the few photographs she had in some small, cheap frames. One of them was a picture of Flo as a child, sitting on a man's lap. She was a beautiful child in a big, lacy dress, just like one of her dolls. I asked the landlady if I could borrow the photograph of Flo. She told me to keep it since nobody else seemed to want it. I took it back with me and put in on the bookcase next to her doll.

JANUARY 30, 1936

Last night I had some real misgivings, so I didn't go back to Tony's. What if the sketch they get from this guy is a good enough likeness that Dennis or Jack sees the similarity? I could be walking into a trap. They could even plant that guy at Tony's who says he remembers me and have him identify me when I walk in. I'm going to stay away from there for a few nights. It's too dangerous.

If Dennis or Jack have any serious suspicions after looking at the sketch, then the police will come here to the office looking for me. There wasn't anything in yesterday's or today's papers. If they had a sketch, wouldn't they publish it right away? What's to be gained by delaying? I wish to hell I knew what was going on. This uncertainty is driving me nuts.

FEBRUARY 3, 1936

I knew when I walked in, from the looks on the guys' faces, that I was in the clear. They said they had been worried about me, wondering why I hadn't been in for several days. I told them I'd been sick with the flu.

Flo never came up in the conversation. Now everyone was talking about the two big killings that happened a few days ago. Richard Loeb, one of the guys who killed that little boy, Bobby Franks, had his throat cut by one of the convicts in prison. Then, last Friday, John Kling, the big industrialist here in Cleveland, was murdered by the chauffeur he had just fired. Events like that make great bar conversation for at least one evening.

I wanted to pump Jack and Dennis about what the police had found out about Flo, but I didn't want to call attention to the subject unless they brought it up first. Since they never brought it up, I'm assuming nothing much is happening. I hope I'm right.

It looks as though I've gotten away with it again. Not that I had any real doubts about my ability to do it. If they haven't found me with that sketch, they'll never find me. It looks like Mr. Ness and his Mr. Cowles aren't all they're cracked up to be, not when they're up against a mind like mine.

[Note: No explanation provided for suspending this volume's entries from February until May of 1936.]

MAY 21, 1936

The weather was just too glorious to stay inside today, so I put on an old suit, put a pint in my pocket, and went for a walk. It's been a long time since I'd been over to Kingsbury Run. I climbed down the slope to where I'd left the two men last September.

A couple hundred yards away were four hobos fixing something to eat over a small fire. They watched me as I approached them, but none of them said a word.

I smiled and said hello and still they didn't answer. Nevertheless, I walked right up to them and introduced myself as Frank. One of them nodded to me, but the others just stared at me as if I had just come down from another planet.

I pulled the pint out of my pocket and took a drink. Still not a sound. I handed it to the guy on my right and asked him if he wanted a drink. He hesitated a second as though it were some kind of trick, but then he took the bottle and had a big gulp.

He was a small, thin fellow, no more than five-foot-four with a scraggly beard and light brown hair. He hadn't had a haircut in quite some time. He smiled and thanked me for the drink and handed me back the pint. Anyone else want some? I asked. They passed it around, and each of them took a healthy swig. That seemed to break the ice.

The small guy on my right told me his name was Johnny. He introduced me to the others. The two big guys in their early twenties were brothers, Orville and Rich. I could tell from their accents they were either from the southern part of the state or West Virginia.

The fourth one was Jim. He was a few inches taller than Johnny but almost as thin. I guessed him to be in his mid-twenties. He was the only one who didn't act friendly after I started passing around my whiskey. He was sizing me up, wondering what the hell I was doing in Kingsbury Run talking to hobos.

Johnny had cooked up some kind of vegetable stew which they ate out of tin cups. They offered me some, but I told them I wasn't hungry. I asked them if it was okay if I sat down with them while they ate. They seemed to be more than happy, especially since I was sharing my whiskey and cigarettes.

As we talked, I learned that the two brothers had come into the city a few days ago from someplace in West Virginia. They heard there were jobs in the mills here and were looking to get some work.

Johnny said that he'd been looking for a job for more than a year and couldn't find anything steady. Just odd jobs. He said that even now with business picking up, the mills weren't doing much new hiring. Mostly they were just going to full-time shifts with the workers they had.

Jim hadn't said a word yet. All the time the three others were talking about looking for work, he looked at them with contempt. Finally, he talked. He said that he hadn't had a job since 1932, and he hoped he'd never have another one.

He'd learned to live off the fat of the land, he said with some pride. Johnny interrupted and said he meant steal the fat off the land. He gave Johnny a threatening look. Hey, shithead, he said to Johnny. Look at you, and then look at me. The difference is I use my brains.

There was some truth in what he said. Jim was by far the least unkempt of the four. His wavy, brown hair was worn a bit long, but he didn't need a haircut. He was clean shaven and looked like he'd found some way to get a shower now and then.

He was wearing a pair of trousers that looked fairly new. The red and blue plaid flannel shirt was a bit rumpled but didn't have any tears or worn spots. He didn't have that down-at-the-heels look the others had.

I asked him what was the secret of living off the fat of the land. He said there was no big mystery to it. When the weather gets cold, he takes a train to Miami or Southern California. As for food and drink, as long as there were lonely women in this world, he'd always have his fill.

And tell him how you get your clothes and money, Johnny blurted out. Jim's cocky expression twisted instantly into a cruel teeth-clenching grimace. He lunged at Johnny and grabbed him by the throat. He told him to shut his fucking mouth, or he'd pull out his tongue.

What a temper. I told him to calm down. I didn't give a rat's ass how he got his money or his clothes. I wasn't a cop or anything.

He threw Johnny back down and grabbed what was left of my pint of whiskey, drinking most of it in one gulp. He said I wouldn't be sitting there if he thought I was a bull, their word for railroad detectives.

Jim said that sometimes the bulls think they're real smart and dress like hobos. He came across one of them in Pittsburgh last summer. The bull, dressed like a hobo, hung around a bunch of them who were waiting to ride the train to Chicago. Jim said he can smell a bull a mile away, no matter how he's dressed or what he says. He came up behind the bull, disarmed him, and beat the shit out of him.

I could tell how much Jim must have enjoyed that. It was the only time I'd seen him smile. He was a lot different than the other three.

The two brothers didn't really belong there. In spite of several days' growth of beard, they looked pretty clean cut and well fed. They were passing through looking for temporary shelter and companionship until they could find some work.

Johnny, even though he looked like he'd been a vagrant all his life, seemed to me to be just another sign of the times. A guy, like so many in the past few years, that's been out of work and thrown into the streets. But I could tell he hated living like that. Once things pick up, as everyone says they will, he'll find some kind of job. Just listening to him talk about what was going on at the mills meant he was looking for work.

Jim, on the other hand, even though he didn't look like a vagrant, was a true hobo. A man who could find work but didn't want to. He seemed to have consciously traded the comfort of a home for the freedom to go anywhere and do anything he wished. At least, on the surface of it, he did well living by his wits.

There was something about Jim I find attractive in a very perverse way, surly as he is. I think it's his dominance I admire. I wish I had more of that in my own personality.

Jim completely controls his life. He makes up his own rules and doesn't have to count on anybody else for his survival. I've always lived by someone else's rules. Even when I break the rules, they're someone else's rules. I'm too dependent on people around me for my survival.

If Jim doesn't like someone, he walks away from them. I can't do that or else I won't have any business. Not only can I not walk away, but I also have to be very nice to patients even if I despise them.

I wonder what Jim's kind of life is really like. Traveling all over the country. Coming and going whenever he pleases. Stealing or conning someone to get the few things he needs. If I were Jim's age, I think I might try that life for a year or two. I'm too old now to even consider living like that and too used to my creature comforts and my whiskey.

MAY 22, 1936

My last patient left at four-thirty this afternoon. I bought another pint of whiskey and went back down to Kingsbury Run. It didn't take long to find Johnny and the two brothers, but Jim wasn't with them. I was disappointed because Jim was the only one I wanted to see.

Johnny suggested I walk down the Run toward town, and I might see him. He pulled me aside out of earshot of the brothers and gave me some advice. He told me I'd better watch myself with Jim, or I'd find myself without my wallet and a lot of ugly bruises instead.

As I walked toward town, the hobo population increased. I passed two small encampments within a mile of each other, but there was no sign of Jim. The smell of their food cooking reminded me I hadn't eaten that afternoon.

Once the sun set, the air got much chillier. The sweater I wore wasn't heavy enough to keep the cold wind from going right through it. I saw another encampment ahead of me with its fire in full blaze. If Jim wasn't there, I was going to warm myself at that fire and start back to the office.

Luck was with me. As I came closer, I spotted Jim's wavy brown hair and red plaid shirt. He was sitting by himself several yards from the fire, drinking some coffee and smoking a cigarette.

He watched me, his face expressionless, as I came over to where he was sitting. I asked him if I could join him. He answered me with a question. Did I bring any whiskey with me? I wonder what he would have said if I hadn't brought any. I think I know. His rudeness amuses me.

I sat down a couple feet away and brought out my pint from my pocket. He took it out of my hand and drank thirstily from it. Then he took one of my cigarettes and lighted it, not reciprocating with any thanks or conversation. I was being tolerated as long as I supplied him with booze and smokes.

For several minutes, we sat without talking, watching the other hobos as they talked and ate whatever it was they had cooked. God knows what it was, but it smelled damned good. I think what they do is bring what they can buy or steal and then throw it all together in a big pot and cook it. That way, everyone who contributes gets something to eat.

It was clear to me that if there was going to be any conversation, it was I who was going to have to initiate it. I told him I found his philosophy and his way of life very intriguing, and I wanted to hear more about it.

He took another gulp of the whiskey and appeared to be thinking about what I said. He asked me if I could see the locomotive on the tracks several hundred yards away. I said yes. He said in twenty minutes, or so, that train was leaving, and he was going to be on it. He was going over to the West Side near the airport. If I wanted to talk to him, I could come along for the ride.

The idea of hopping a freight train, even if it was just to ride across town, was pretty heady stuff for me. Then I wondered if I could do it. I'm really out of shape for that kind of activity. But, shit, how would I have ever known if I could or couldn't unless I gave it a try.

I said I'd go with him, but I'd never hopped a train before and needed him to give me some pointers. He grunted which I took to mean he would. A few minutes later, he stood up, and I followed him as he walked along the tracks away from the train. We had to hop on the train when it was still moving slowly, but when the train was far enough away from the yard, so the bulls didn't see us.

It was very dark as we walked along the tracks. There was hardly any moonlight, and I couldn't see well at all. Some twenty yards away, we stopped, and he told me what to do when the train came by.

Suddenly, there was a blinding glare as the light on the locomotive shone down the tracks. The train was getting ready to leave the yard. Next, I heard the sound of the whistle and then the clacking of the wheels getting closer and closer. My heart was beating wildly as I anticipated what I had to do in the next couple minutes.

Jim must have seen the terror on my face in the white glare of the train. He told me not to worry, just do what he said. That didn't give me much comfort. Jim is not the kind of person a thinking man puts a lot of trust in. Were I to fall to my death under the wheels of the train, Jim wouldn't give a shit. But I had no other mentor and too much pride to back out, having already come that far.

We stood back from the tracks in the shadows until the locomotive and first few cars went by us. Then Jim saw his opportunity and sprung into motion. We started to run alongside the train.

He grabbed the side of the door of an open boxcar and swung his body up into the car in one graceful motion. As I ran, he held out one of his hands to me. I grabbed it and the side of the boxcar and made the jump. I could never have done it if he hadn't been pulling me up. Thank God, he was strong. It couldn't have been easy for him to pull up someone my size.

Once I made it into the boxcar, I sat there for quite a few minutes trying to catch my breath. Jim just laughed at me. I thought to myself, enjoy this, Frank, it's something you're only going to do once in your life.

After a few minutes, I got to my feet and stood near Jim at the open door of the car. The train started to pick up some speed. It was really quite beautiful watching the lights of the city as we passed them by. The cold breeze blew steadily in my face, and I felt a wonderful sense of freedom. I could see where it could become addictive.

Jim sat down at the far end of the boxcar while I stood at the door and watched until the lights of the city gave way to the dark woods of the Cuyahoga River Valley. We had turned south from Kingsbury Run, following the river. Eventually, we turned west, and Jim got up briefly to see where we were. He pointed out the zoo to me and told me the train was going to slow down soon.

As the train slowed, he motioned to me. That's where we would get off. This time, it wasn't so easy. The train wasn't going as slowly as when we got on. It was very dark, and I could barely see the ground. He jumped and left me to decide for myself. I hesitated. There are times when being a doctor is a disadvantage. I've already treated the results of people jumping off things they shouldn't.

I made a hard landing, twisting my ankle in the process. I limped over to Jim who was some thirty yards away. He said there was a camp close by. We walked about a quarter of a mile along the tracks. My ankle was killing me.

I didn't see any camp fires ahead and wondered if Jim knew where he was going. Maybe Johnny was right. This was where Jim would hit me on the head and take my wallet. Eventually, we reached the place he was talking about, except that no one else was there. We're on our own, he said. The two of us had to gather up some sticks for a fire.

Once we had the fire going, Jim unrolled his pack, took out some beef jerky and a good-sized knife to cut pieces of beef for the two of us.

I asked him if he was going to spend the night here. He said he was going to sleep with a woman he found last week who lives close by. He just had to wait until later when her husband left for the night shift at the mill. Then tomorrow, he'd hop the train to Chicago.

I asked him about the woman he was going to see tonight. Was she good looking? He said he doesn't care if a woman's attractive as long as she gives him a place to sleep.

Good looking women expect to get something from a man, he explained to me, as though I had just fallen off the turnip truck. Whereas plainer women are very generous if you give them some attention. Jim said when he wants a place to stay for the night, he goes into a bar and looks around for a woman who's plain or overweight. Then he finds out if she has someplace where he can stay. If she doesn't, he talks to her for another minute or two and tries another girl.

He said every once in a while, he gets real lucky and finds a woman with a lot of cash on her. Then he makes sure that he gets up real early, takes her cash, and slips out before she knows he's gone.

Women are so easy to put things over on, he told me with his cocky smile. He said he could get anything they had just by pretending he's attracted to them.

As he talked, I watched his face in the firelight. When he spoke about something he liked, his face was so different than the sullen expression I'd seen before. His large eyes could be very expressive, and his smile, when it wasn't curled into a sneer, was quite attractive. I could see where he would be very successful with women when he wanted to be.

The heat from the fire was becoming very intense. Jim stood up and took off his jacket. His slim, muscular body was accented by his tight-fitting denim pants. A body conditioned to fighting and fucking, the ultimate expression of his strong will.

In retrospect, it may have been my subconscious intention all along to possess him. I guess I only realized it then as he stood in front of me before the fire. My mind started to grasp at the thread of opportunity and the stark practicalities of execution.

This man presented more challenge to me than any of the others. He was strong and quick. Even though I am larger and heavier, his strength was probably equal to mine. It had to be with my wits that I took him.

When he sat down, I handed him my whiskey and told him to take what he wanted while I gathered up some more wood for the fire. My biggest advantage was that he was not on his guard around me. Ironically, he may have even been looking at me as his prey.

I picked up wood and put some of it on the fire. The rest I stacked next to him. When out of the corner of my eye I saw that he was reaching again for the whiskey, I knew the opportunity had come. I started to walk slowly around in back of him to the place where I had been sitting before.

As he cocked his head back to take a swig of the whiskey, I threw my whole weight into my arm choke, reaching down and grabbing his knife with my other hand.

He struggled like a son of a bitch, trying to pull my arm from his throat. He clawed at me and knocked the knife out of my hand. We rolled around on the ground. Finally, my weight worked in my favor, and I pinned him face down on the ground, my knee firmly in his back. I pulled his head back by the hair and pressed my arm tight against his windpipe. I felt him weakening against me. Then gradually he stopped fighting me. He was mine.

While he lay there unconscious, I stripped off my shirt. I still had to get back to my office, and I couldn't do that safely if I had blood all over me.

I found his knife on the ground. It was much smaller than the one I was used to. It wouldn't do the job as neatly as I liked, but it was all I had.

There was something in the setting there, perhaps the firelight, that made it so much more intimate than my surgery. My hands trembled with excitement as I made the long, clean cut. Once again I felt the rush of power as his life flowed out in front of me. Everything he was is now taken into me.

I was exhausted and exhilarated at the same time. All I wanted to do was to sleep and dream, but I put my shirt and sweater back on and sat for a while enjoying the last glowing vestiges of the fire. I still had a long night ahead of me.

Finally, I summoned up all my strength and dragged him by the feet into the wooded area some fifty yards away. I covered him with his jacket and wool blanket and hoped that it would be at least a few days before someone found him. Too many people had seen me with him at the hobo camp.

I took one last look around and started walking toward the nearest lights of civilization. It took me the rest of the evening to get back to my office, waiting for buses, transferring to other buses.

But in all the time it took me to get back, I had my second wind. I walked over to the small diner on 55th Street and went in. I was ravenously hungry.

[Note: No explanation for gap in journal entries between May 22 and June 2 in this volume.]

JUNE 2, 1936

After what happened this morning, I've got to stop drinking so damned much. As I lay blissfully sleeping on my couch, I felt the wonderful sensation of my penis being stroked by some unknown hand. What a marvelous dream I thought as I gradually awakened. For a few moments, I just lay there reveling in the exquisite feeling, slowly realizing that it was not a dream after all.

I was horrified when I opened my eyes to find a naked guy kneeling next to the couch with his hand upon me. Worse, he was grinning as though I should be pleased!

I yanked his hand off me, almost breaking it in the process, and demanded to know how the hell he had gotten in my office. Lying faggot tried to make me believe I owed him twenty bucks for a blow job last night. Now I might have offered him a place to sleep. I was so plastered I don't remember, but I wouldn't have if I'd known he was queer.

That boy's sucked his last cock! I was so angry, I dragged him into the surgery, grabbed the first knife I found and cut his goddamn throat, letting him bleed into the sink. There was no pleasure in it. He made my skin crawl. I felt sick inside and dirty from touching him. I finished the job and wrapped his head in his trousers so I wouldn't have to look at his face anymore.

That's when I noticed his clothes. New cashmere trousers and an expensive white shirt. Jesus Christ, he was better dressed than I was. I wonder who the hell this guy was. It's strange. Those good clothes don't fit with the rest of him, particularly the tattoos. I don't understand why a pretty boy queer would get six tattoos.

JUNE 3, 1936

I don't know why I create such problems for myself. Now, I have to get rid of him. I'm taking too many chances. Only have one patient coming in tomorrow, so I can hide him until tomorrow night and then figure out where to take him.

Why not Kingsbury Run? Things there had quieted down considerably. For now, I'll just take his head down to the car. No, I'll wait until it's safe and get his body out to the car tonight. There's something about him that gives me the creeps.

JUNE 4, 1936

Whew. Nothing like what a warm day or two can add to a stiff. I rolled down the windows, so I didn't choke.

When I got near the Run, I drove down and parked the car near the tracks. The area looked deserted, but the lights were on in the office of the Nickel Plate Railroad police. Three guys inside having a great time drinking beer and playing cards. This was almost too good to be true. Maybe I would get some enjoyment out of this after all.

I looked around again and got his head out of the trunk, still wrapped up tight in his trousers. I carried it to the bushes just in front of the building, unwrapped him, and ran like the devil back to my car. I waited and watched until it was clear nobody saw me then I carried his body and hid it under some bushes not too far away.

God, how I wish I could be there when they find him.

JUNE 6, 1936

It's great to be back in the news again. I'd forgotten how much pleasure it gives me. Lots of front page stuff.

I went back to Tony's tonight, but only Hanley was there. Both Jack and Dennis had this Saturday night off. Hanley said Hogan sees no connection between this latest death and any of the others. I find that absolutely incredible. I can understand where Hogan might not necessarily see the connection between the bodies in Kingsbury Run and Flo or the Lady of the Lake, but you'd have to be a real idiot not to figure out that I did Andrassy and this young queer, who Hanley has christened the Tattooed Man.

Hogan is all excited because he's sure they can identify the kid because of the good condition of his body and the distinctive tattoos. I'm not so sure. If this boy was a prostitute, nobody's going to step forward to associate themselves with him. Then, maybe he's from out of town and just came in for the Republican Convention to make some influential friends.

Hanley says Ness wants the body on display at the morgue the next few days for anybody to come in and look at it. I guess I am flattered that Ness is paying so much attention to my work, but it sounds so ghoulish to put the dead on public display. Whatever happened to good taste?

JUNE 7, 1936

I've never seen anything like it. There must have been a thousand people crowding into the morgue to get a glimpse of him. They had both the head and body displayed to show all the tattoos.

It was an eerie experience, looking again at his young face. His huge blue eyes had been closed of course, and it looked like he was sleeping peacefully. It made me sad things had turned out that way. I really have to control my temper.

I was appalled at the way people were pushing and shoving to get a better look at him. And some of the comments they made. How would they feel if this was their son or brother? This is the same crowd that would come to public executions if they still had them.

JUNE 8, 1936

I suppose to make my point once and for all, I could kill someone else and stick the body down in the Run, but it would be much too dangerous so soon after this last one. The Run is just crawling with cops and railroad detectives. I think I'll just wait a few weeks until things cool off.

[Note: June 8, 1936, is the final entry on the last page of this volume. September 8, 1936, is the first entry in a new volume. No explanation is given as to whether a missing intervening volume exists.]

SEPTEMBER 8, 1936

I'm hoping enough time has passed so it really is safe now for me to indulge myself again. Now that they found Jim the hobo's body, the clever Mr. Hogan deduced that one person is responsible. It's taken me more than a year and seven deaths to make that one point. They've all been so clever, I've decided to reward these intellectual giants with my latest plaything.

SEPTEMBER 10, 1936

They found his head late this morning. I could hear the police sirens from my office around noon, so I turned on the radio to hear the news. I desperately wanted to go over to Kingsbury Run, but I had two patients coming in the early afternoon.

I wasn't able to get over there until almost four-thirty, and when I did, I was astonished. I've never seen that area so jammed. I suppose I shouldn't complain. After all, the crowds were there because I brought them there.

I do believe that there were more cops in Kingsbury Run than Mr. Ness had assembled for his famous raid on the Harvard Club earlier this year. The whole ravine was alive with photographers, newspapermen, cops, and spectators. Taking pictures of every-thing in sight, the Run, the hobos, the police. I think I have put that sorry place on the map.

Hanley was there, talking to one of the cops. I asked him what was going on, and he told me that some hobo had stumbled over half of the torso when he was running to catch a train. The police had found the other half nearby. The body must have washed down from the sewers that drained the pool I dumped him in.

I saw Jack there working. I waved to him, but he didn't see me. I didn't go any closer, not wanting to disturb him while he was right there under Hogan's nose. He was fishing around with a grappling hook in the pool underneath the bridge. Poor guy. He had to stand balanced on a board they had placed across the pool and search for the missing pieces. One wrong step and he would have fallen into the awful-smelling sewer water. Not a very nice way to spend the afternoon.

Hanley wanted to do a special story on how these murders were affecting the people in the area, both the residents and the hobos. I followed him around as he talked to people. First, we walked over to a small group of hobos and asked them what they thought of the latest killing. Two of them said they were going to catch a freight out of the city tonight. It wasn't safe for them in the city anymore.

One of the hobos confided to us that he knows who the killer is. He whispered that there's a big hobo named Vince who lives in the Flats. All the hobos are afraid of him. He carries a knife and has threatened some of the hobos he was going to cut them up.

I asked the hobo if he'd ever seen Vince. He told me that everyone there had seen Vince. He was big, real big, with long, dark brown hair and a long beard. I said that description fit hun-dreds of hobos. How would I ever know this Vince if I ran into him? He told me it was Vince's eyes I should look for. Big, crazy eyes, like a madman. Hanley was enthralled by Vince. He said he was going to tell Jack about him so he could go along when Jack picked him up.

Another hobo told us he was going to stay in the city. He heard the killings were all faked as part of a plot by the mayor and the railroads to scare all the hobos out of town. But, he showed us a pretty good-sized knife he was carrying for protection just in case the railroad detectives were killing hobos instead of getting the dead bodies from the morgue.

For the most part, they're really frightened, these hobos are. Sleeping out there in the open every night, so vulnerable and exposed. The ones who stay here will probably huddle closer together now. Go places in groups instead of walking around alone.

We talked to some of the other spectators, the ones who live and work at the top of the ravine. One woman who had just arrived, scurried back home when she heard what had happened to make sure her children were safe in the house. The man next to her was talking about the dog he was going to buy tomorrow so that no maniac got near his house.

Another woman we talked to told me she was going to tell the police about the strange man who had moved in several houses away from her. A couple of nights ago, she saw him carrying suspicious packages out of his house to his car. She was going to have her husband put another bolt on the door before he went to work tonight.

I'm fascinated by the fear that has seized these solid, practical working class people who live around here. They're not exposed like the hobos. They have locks on their doors and neighbors around them, yet there is clearly a feeling of panic. I have touched the lives of each of them.

And the police. I can't forget about them. At least for now, their lives are the most directly affected by my work. The poor stupid slobs are still obsessed with trying to identify the dead man. As though it would do them any good. They still haven't learned yet that I deliberately don't get to know the people I kill.

So, on they go, blindly following the same paths that led to failure before. Tracking down every clue to his identity. I swear to God, I'd call up the police department with his name and address if I knew it, just so they could realize it doesn't make any difference who he was, anymore than it did with Andrassy or Flo.

It's very clear to me that the collective IQ of the cops working on this case doesn't match up to the intelligence I have in my little toe. Their illustrious leader Eliot Ness, on whose intellect I will reserve judgment, is too damn busy closing down gambling joints to match wits with me.

We stayed around for several hours. The police were starting to leave, and the crowd of spectators was dwindling rapidly. Nobody wants to be in Kingsbury Run after dark anymore.

I felt pretty good and wanted to share my high spirits with someone else. I told Hanley I'd buy him a drink, so we went over to Tony's. I looked around for Dennis and Jack, but neither was there. In fact, Tony's was almost empty. I asked Tony why, and he said Eliot Ness had everyone in the Third Precinct working overtime on the new murder case. How ironic, there I was, ready to celebrate my fame, and everybody I wanted to celebrate with was busy working on the case. At least I had Hanley for an hour or so before he had to leave.

Hanley is fascinated by what I've done. He feels that there is some special significance that all the people I killed were from the lowest levels of society. Hanley thinks the killer is some wealthy psychopath who kills the lower classes for sport. I had to laugh. I couldn't help it. It sounded so feudal.

I told him I didn't buy his theory. I said that the killer's way of selecting people was probably a practical matter. He may live among the prostitutes and drifters and find them the most accessible.

We stayed there for another hour or so until Hanley had to go work on his story. After I came back to the office, I got to thinking about our conversation. I wish I understood why I get such a feeling of power when I kill those people. I can't imagine why it seems like such a victory to me. How can killing such losers be a victory over anything?

I suppose the psychologists would say the answer is somewhere in my childhood. And what a miserable childhood it was, living in terror of my father. But I've overcome that now. I'm no longer the powerless victim I was when I was young.

How I hated that man. Even in the poor neighborhood where we lived, I was so ashamed of him. Everybody made fun of him as he stumbled home drunk. Maybe it's him that I'm killing over and over. No, that's ridiculous.

The answer could be that I simply need power. I started out craving that ultimate life and death power over a person. Now that I have experienced it to the fullest, it's not nearly as exciting as having power over an entire city like I have right now.

One result, although I hadn't thought about it until now, of killing the kind of people that I do, is the attention stays focused on the killing and not on the person killed. I must make sure that no one else in the future can be identified. That way, my audience won't be distracted by an ocean of sordid biographical trivia like they printed about Andrassy and Flo. I want the newspapers to stay focused on what I did, not the people I killed.

I think that's fair. None of those pathetic creatures could have ever hoped to receive the level of public attention I have fashioned for them with my knife. Like an artist, I have taken human trash nobody cares about, or should care about for that matter, and created excitement, mystery, and drama, which has captivated this entire city.

SEPTEMBER 11, 1936

I have finally arrived. Not only have I made the front page again, but I have completely taken it over. At last, I am somebody in this city.

I can't say that I'm real pleased with the name Hanley has given me in his article. The Mad Butcher of Kingsbury Run. It is kind of funny though when I think of them looking for a wild-eyed maniac in a long, white apron, brandishing a butcher knife. Whatever happened to that dramatic flair of Hanley's when he named my first whore the Lady of the Lake?

The paper said the police department switchboards have been jammed with calls from people reporting the suspicious behavior of their relatives and neighbors. Eliot Ness has ordered a special telephone number for people to call in with tips.

After I had read the paper this morning, I turned on the radio. The police told people to stay away from Kingsbury Run since the traffic was so jammed up. There were already over a thousand people watching the police drag that pool. I'll be damned. A thousand people would come to watch them fishing in a pool of stagnant water.

I don't often do this, write more than once in a day, but today was so wonderful, I wanted to capture my feelings before they slipped away.

When I walked over to Kingsbury Run, it was mobbed. If there were a thousand people there this morning, the number had easily doubled by this afternoon. I'm drawing larger crowds than the Great Lakes Exposition.

The evening paper gave three pages of coverage to me. There were pictures of where all the bodies had been found and photos of Andrassy and Flo. The article said reporters were coming in from New York, Chicago, Washington, and even London, England, to write stories about the murders. There has never been anything like this case in the whole country.

The papers are comparing me to Jack the Ripper and somebody named Henri Landru, who killed eleven women in France in the 1920's. I didn't realize Jack the Ripper had only killed five prostitutes. How did he get so famous killing only five whores?

I'm sure it's the mystery of it that fascinates everyone. The unknown phantom who kills in the night. It strikes a chord in all of us. That's why Jack the Ripper is so famous and that Landru guy isn't. Jack the Ripper lives as a frightening legend, undiminished by facts and photographs of him. Whereas Landru, even though he killed twice as many people as the Ripper, was caught and the mystery was solved. His life was dissected, analyzed, and put into a file somewhere. Case closed. I had never even heard of the guy.

It's thrilling to think that soon the whole world may be reading about what I've accomplished. If only Hanley had come up with some better name than The Mad Butcher. It has no style to it. Maybe I can suggest some other phrase to Hanley before this Mad Butcher idea gets too entrenched in people's minds.

I went to Dugan's tonight. Everybody in there was talking about Kingsbury Run. Bertie and Driscoll had walked over there this morning to watch the police, but they left when they saw Mullens there. So even Mullens couldn't stay away. That makes me happy. Wouldn't he be terrified if he knew it was me behind all this excitement? He's damn lucky it's not his body in the pool.

Driscoll said the nurses are scared to death to wait for buses in the dark, so the hospital is going to put in some more lighting all around the grounds. They're going to have orderlies escort the nurses out to the bus stops and wait there with them.

Mullens told Driscoll he was worried that all the publicity about Kingsbury Run would scare away new patients. Already, the patients were complaining that nobody would visit them because they were afraid to go anywhere near the area.

It gives me so much pleasure to sit among my friends and listen to them talk about all the excitement I have created. The irony of it tickles me. They postulate their half-baked theories about the killer when I sit there in the midst of them. It would never occur to them it was Frank, the person they think they know so well.

SEPTEMBER 12, 1936

Kingsbury Run was like a circus today. There must have been five thousand people. Street vendors were selling peanuts and hot dogs, and young boys were charging twenty-five cents for a guided tour of where the bodies had been found.

The police had hired a diver who spent the day looking for the missing parts. Early today, they found the thighs and lower legs. That's all they are going to find, no matter how long they look, because I dumped the head and the arms into the lake, way east of the city, wrapped in a burlap bag, weighted down with rocks.

We stopped to talk to one of the railroad cops Hanley knew. He said the hobos were leaving Kingsbury Run by the dozens. The railroad police had spread the word that they had relaxed their usual searches of the cars going out of the city. They wanted to encourage as many of them as possible to leave.

When it started to get dark, we went back to Tony's and found Dennis finishing his supper. He was really pissed that he had to work on his day off. He said that the station was a complete mad-house. It seemed to him that everybody in the city knew who the killer might be. The phone hadn't stopped ringing all day, and it was driving him nuts. Eliot Ness ordered every lead to be followed up, no matter how stupid or trivial.

Hanley and I went back with Dennis to take a look. On the first floor, there was a huge crowd of people waiting to give the police their tips. These people had tried unsuccessfully to get through to the station on the phone, and when that didn't work, they came in person. We pushed our way through the crowd and followed Dennis to the steps leading to the basement. There was a patrolman there on guard making sure that only authorized people passed.

We followed Dennis downstairs to a big double door where there were two other patrolmen standing guard. Dennis opened the door and let us take a look inside.

I guess I wasn't prepared to see a whole rag-tag army of sus-pects wall-to-wall inside the room. The room was not nearly large enough to hold the hundred or more people enclosed in there. I saw a couple of them urinating over in the corner of the room. No wonder it smelled so bad. And the cigarette smoke was so thick, I could hardly see the back of the room. There weren't more than a handful of chairs, so practically everybody was either standing up against the walls or sitting on the floor. A few of them had found enough room to stretch out and go to sleep.

It would take them days to question all those men. Dennis said there were even more at the central station downtown. The detec-tives just kept bringing them in. I could see now how Hogan was using his twenty-five detectives on this case.

Hanley and I went back over to Tony's and drank for another hour. Then he had to leave and get started on his article for the morning paper. I was in such good spirits that I went over to Dugan's and spent the rest of the evening with my friends over there.

SEPTEMBER 13, 1936

As I read the newspaper today, it looked as though Eliot Ness has upstaged me with my own publicity. He's finally realized how much public interest there is in the case and tried to turn it to his own advantage. I think it may have backfired on him, though.

Just after dark last night, he sent down a bunch of cops to arrest all the hobos in that whole section of Kingsbury Run where the bodies had been found. The cops loaded dozens of them in paddy wagons, took them all down to Central Station, and arrested them. Bless my soul, if my dear cousin didn't get in on the act too. Somebody called up Martin on the phone last night and asked him to comment on what Ness did. Martin did more than that. He got in his car and went down to the station to see for himself.

In the interview, Martin blasted Ness. He called the raid a blatant disregard for the rights of the poor and disadvantaged. Ness was creating a police state atmosphere by a senseless mass arrest of a group of wretched souls. Worse than that, Martin said, the poor vagrants were being held in a detention room without any sanitary facilities. Martin charged Ness with using the arrests to draw attention away from the fact he had allowed a mad killer to roam the streets for over a year.

SEPTEMBER 14, 1936

Eliot and I made the papers again today. He denied the rumor that he had taken control of the Kingsbury Run case. He said that he's put his Assistant Safety Director in charge. That's odd. I had been given the impression that Ness was pulling all the strings himself.

I went over to Tony's tonight. Jack was there for a change, looking completely exhausted. He told me that this was the first free evening he's had since they found that recent body in Kingsbury Run.

I asked him if they had any good leads yet. He said he sure didn't know of any. They didn't have much to go on unless they were able to find the dead man's hands and head. Without some way to identify the man, they would strike out once again. They never learn, I thought to myself as I heard that comment.

Jack said they were still chasing down the hundreds of tips people had given them. Then they had to question and fingerprint all the characters they'd picked up. It would take them another week or two to finish up what they had.

Jack was hiding out in Tony's so that his new partner, a guy named Pete, didn't find him. He told me that none of the other detectives would work with Pete because he was such a nut. Jack got the honors since he was the low man on the totem pole.

He said that this Pete was completely obsessed with these murders. He worked from real early in the morning until after midnight every night chasing down weirdos, even on his night off. Jack told him to go out tonight by himself because he was going to rest.

Jack's partner must be a real pain in the ass. The night before they had worked until one in the morning. Then, when Jack finally got to sleep around one thirty, Pete called him and told him to get dressed because he needed help in bringing in some big hobo for questioning.

Hanley asked Jack what he thought about the meeting last night with Eliot Ness. Apparently, there had been some big pow-wow at Central Station. All the key people working on the case were there to compare what they knew about the killings. Jack said that after they had reviewed all the information they had on the murders, they didn't have any more to go on than they had when the murders started.

I asked Jack what Eliot Ness thought of the case. Had he really turned it over to his assistant? Jack didn't know for sure, but Ness seemed to be annoyed by the whole thing. He told all of them he wanted the case wrapped up right away so the department could get on to more important things.

Hanley said he'd heard the same thing. Rumor was the mayor told Ness he better get the case solved because it was an embarrassment to the administration, but Ness didn't want to shelve his pet project, the police department investigation, to work on some murder case.

So the newspaper was right. Eliot Ness is too busy to give me any more of his time. That's a decision he'll live to regret. I ought to put the next goddamn body right on his front steps. Although, I'm not so sure that it would make a difference.

He must have an odd set of values. Here is a murder case of national interest right here in his backyard. Instead of throwing himself into it, he prefers to spend all his time cleaning up his dirty little police department.

For someone who is such a publicity hound, I find his behavior most unusual. Those reporters from New York and London must be writing stories for their papers. Ness's police department investigation will never get that kind of coverage outside of this city.

Maybe he's the kind of person who only gets involved with things he can control. He knows he can't control me. He doesn't even have a clue about how to catch me. In fact, I'm the one who's in control, not him. He and the police department only respond to what I do. I set their pace.

I think I'm beginning to understand why Ness is putting some distance between himself and this case. From everything I had seen and heard about him, he wants to see quick results from what he does.

I think Jack may have summed it up. The police have nothing to show for the thousands of hours they've put into this investigation. All these silly little clues and vague suspicions, all the hundreds of weirdos they have locked up, all of it will lead nowhere. That must drive Eliot Ness nuts.

SEPTEMBER 15, 1936

I was quite surprised to see the Plain Dealer this morning. I had been getting the feeling this investigation was starting to wind down again. I was dead wrong. The major headline on the front page was the coroner calling me a new insane type. That certainly got my attention.

The article went all the way to the bottom of the first page and was continued beyond that on another page. What generated it was the meeting the coroner called Monday night to review the facts of the case. I didn't realize last night when Jack and Hanley were talking just what a big meeting it was.

The coroner had called in the county pathologist, two anatomy professors, the court psychiatrist, the head guy in an insane asylum, Eliot Ness, Hogan, Cullitan, the county prosecutor from the Harvard Club raid, and some of the cops working on the case. After several hours, they came to seven conclusions, some of which are idiotically obvious.

The best one was that they finally realized that the killings are the work of one man. The article didn't say anything about how long it took them to figure that out. Another startling conclusion was that the victims were all from the lower classes. Excellent police deductive powers. Next, they concluded that I was big and strong. That's pretty clear, considering I carried those bodies down Jackass Hill into Kingsbury Run. Ness said I have the strength of an ox, a left-handed compliment if I ever heard one.

They also decided that even though I am obviously demented that I may not be recognizably insane. I am apparently a new kind of unique nut. Very good. I wonder what they would think if they knew I spent my evenings conversing with cops and a newspaperman. I'm not anymore obviously demented than they are.

Then they pissed me off. They saw no evidence that I had any medical training. I find that absolutely unbelievable. They decided the knowledge of anatomy indicated I was a butcher or a hunter, not a physician.

I was furious and threw the paper across the room. Eventually, I calmed down and thought about it. Their ignorance works in my favor. The worst thing that could happen right now is that the coroner decides the killer is a surgeon. Boy, would that put the heat on me. So, I guess, I am somewhat grateful for their stupidity. It helps keep me out of the electric chair.

The more I think about it, the more I can see why they would suspect a butcher rather than a doctor. Doctors, even surgeons, don't have any real experience in cutting people into pieces. They don't do that in the normal course of their work. Once in a while, I had an amputation, but that was uncommon. There would be no reason to assume that a surgeon would be proficient in decapitating someone.

On the other hand, a butcher cuts bodies apart for a living. Even though he isn't familiar with human anatomy, he could become reasonably expert in cutting apart a human body in a short time based on his experience with animal carcasses. Maybe it's not as dumb as I first thought.

Their last two conclusions make me more than a little nervous. They believe I live in or near Kingsbury Run, and I have a workshop where I could kill without being discovered.

Damn. I should never have put four of them in that one spot. I should have known that putting so many of them in Kingsbury Run would draw too much attention to this neighborhood. For someone as smart as I am, I sure do some stupid things. One thing for sure, that's the last body I'm going to put in Kingsbury Run.

SEPTEMBER 16, 1936

I stopped over to see Agnes this morning. I had a couple of hours free before my first patient. It had been almost two weeks since I'd seen her.

There were some things weighing heavily on my mind that I had to talk over with her. Things we both experienced when we were growing up.

As close as Agnes and I have always been, we never really talked much about our childhood. How it affected us. I don't quite know why we never talked about it. Perhaps until now, it didn't seem important to discuss. Or maybe it's a holdover from what Sis drilled into us as kids.

All the time we were growing up, Sis impressed on us that we were never to talk to anybody about Father's drinking or his violence. Not to our friends or our teachers, not even our cousins. I don't think that Agnes or I ever questioned Sis's Rule of Silence; we just obeyed it as best we could.

As I look back on it, I think Sis was trying to protect our family from the shame his drinking brought down on us. It was so embarrassing to have all the neighbors talking about the things he did in public, like pissing in the front yard one summer evening when everybody was outside to see it. At least we could be quiet about the things he did in private.

After all those years of silence, I had to talk to Agnes about it. I had to know how it affected her. Then perhaps, I can understand better how it has affected me.

It wasn't easy getting Agnes to talk. Forget it, she told me. It's in the past. It's over and done with, she insisted. Besides, she said, it was wrong to speak ill of the dead. I told her I didn't want to talk about Father. There was no point in it. I wanted to talk about us. I promised her that if she talked to me just this once, I'd never bring it up again.

I told her I was trying to remember exactly how I felt when Father got so violent. When he'd beat us over the slightest little thing. I wanted to know how she felt when that happened. Was she angry? Was she sad? Did she feel guilty?

Agnes said she remembers Father used to hit her, but she couldn't remember the details much. She said she had done as much as she could to block it out of her memory. All she could tell me was she felt numb like she'd shut herself down emotionally.

I told her I often felt that way too. I said it was almost like an emotional state of shock, like the physical shock that happens when a person is severely injured. Except our emotional shock was chronic. It was an everyday part of our lives when we were in that house.

I remembered how happy I was when I was fourteen and got a job loading boxes at the plant a few blocks away. It was a difficult job, and every cent I made went right to Sis for essentials, but it gave me a reason for not coming home after school. It was my only release from the tension of living there.

But Agnes had to come home right after school and help Sis. The two of them had to deal with Father for much of the day. Then she quit school when she was eleven or twelve and did little odd jobs for the stores and restaurants on Broadway.

And then, when Sis got married, Agnes had to take care of Father all by herself while I worked. It must have been awful for her, spending so much time in that house with him.

I asked her if she felt that we were different from other people because of what we'd gone through as kids. I expected her to say no, but she didn't say anything. She got up from the table and made some more coffee. From the look on her face, she was thinking hard about my question.

Agnes came back to the table and sat down again. She sat there for a few minutes in silence. Then she sighed. I could tell she didn't like these soul-searching conversations.

She started out by saying she didn't know how the rest of us were affected, but she felt she was different from other people. She wasn't sure whether to blame Father for it or not.

Agnes said it was difficult to describe, this difference that she felt. She had never tried to put it into words before, but she didn't think she was normal emotionally. She said it wasn't anything other people would notice, but she was very aware of it.

She said she didn't have the same depth of feeling other people had. When people around her cried at funerals, she didn't feel any grief. When others were happy at weddings and birthday parties, she felt nothing. It was as though she was completely covered with a hard shell. Emotions didn't get in, and emotions didn't get out.

She said the craziest thing about it was that it was different with animals. She told me she cried for days when the dog next door got killed by a car. She said she felt worse about the dog than when our brother John got sick and died. She begged me never to tell that to anyone.

She said she wished she could make herself be like everyone else, but she couldn't. She just wasn't normal. It was like there was something dead in her soul.

Agnes said there was something else that made her feel different from other people, something inside her that kept her from getting too close to anybody. Even Lee, she said. She didn't get real angry when he treated her badly, and she didn't feel anything when he treated her well. She didn't love him, and she didn't hate him. She just lived with him.

And it wasn't just Lee either, she said. She felt that way about most everybody, even Sis. Then she started to get all teary and reached across the table and held my hand. She said that I was the only person in the world she felt close to. The only people she felt she really loved were Patricia and me.

I held on to her hand and told her I understood more than she realized. I said she was the only person I'd ever felt love for, except for Mama and my boys.

As painful as it was for her to look into herself, I think she was relieved to finally talk to someone about it. A relief I will never have. How strange it is that we who are so close have kept so many important secrets from each other.

SEPTEMBER 17, 1936

Last night was one of the most enjoyable nights I have had in a long time. It started at Tony's with a terrific plate of spaghetti and meatballs. Jack and Dennis were there with me too, eating their dinners.

Jack was very tired. He had deep circles under his eyes. He sat there quietly and ate his sandwich while Dennis and I talked about what to do with Dennis's bad shoulder.

I told Jack I didn't see him in Tony's much anymore. What was it that kept him away, his partner, or his girlfriend? He sighed and said he wished it was his girlfriend.

Dennis laughed and teased him about his partner. Dennis said Pete was becoming the laughing stock of the department. He urged Jack to tell me the latest Pete story, but Jack didn't want to talk about it anymore. Dennis kept egging him on, saying he couldn't do the story justice himself.

Finally, Jack agreed, but only if I bought him another beer, which I did. This was obviously a story Jack had told a number of times recently, and he had to get himself geared up to tell it right. He took a couple of swigs of his beer, and a big smile spread across his face.

Jack said it had all started with the big meeting Eliot Ness had with the coroner and a number of the detectives, right after they found the last body in Kingsbury Run. During that meeting, while they were theorizing on how to catch the killer, Coroner Pearse had come up with an idea. Why not have the police dress up as hobos and mingle among them in Kingsbury Run late at night? Maybe they could bait the killer into attacking one of them.

Everybody in the room laughed at the coroner's silly suggestion, except Pete, who thought it was a great idea. Fortunately, Pete and Jack had been so busy chasing down leads people had called in, that Pete didn't have time to try out the idea.

Last night, Pete told Jack to dress like a hobo, and they would go down to Kingsbury Run around eleven o'clock. Pete picked him up, and they drove down to the area where the latest body was found.

Jack said it was fairly quiet down there, with only a few hobo fires burning. Pete searched around and found a spot by the railroad tracks, a distance away from the nearest hobo camp. He pointed to some big sumac bushes and told Jack to hide behind them. Jack was to keep an eye on him while Pete walked up and down the railroad tracks.

Then his partner started to take off his clothes. Jack asked him what the hell he was doing taking his clothes off in Kingsbury Run. As he stripped down to his underwear, Pete explained that since the killer was a sex pervert, the way to attract him was to walk around in his underwear.

Jack wished he had a picture of the short fat man with his big stomach protruding as he paraded up and down the tracks in his long johns. After this had been going on for about twenty minutes, he heard two hobos coming toward them. When the hobos saw the eerie figure in white long underwear walking in the moonlight, they were scared and ran off.

Dennis and I started to laugh, but Jack stopped us. Wait, he said, it gets better. He said that Pete walked along the tracks for another half hour when he saw several flashlights coming toward Pete. Then all of a sudden, about twelve men converged on Pete with their guns drawn. The hobos had called the railroad detectives who had moved in to capture the nut who was walking around in his underwear. Jack watched as Pete struggled and tried to break free. The railroad police had wrestled him down to the ground. By then, a couple dozen hobos had gathered around closer to watch the arrest.

Jack was absolutely mortified when he had to explain to the railroad police that this was his partner. He said that the railroad detectives just hooted at Pete when they found out who he was. Even the hobos were whistling and making cute little noises at him. It should have been a very humbling experience for Pete, but apparently, it wasn't. Jack said Pete is so hard-headed that he wanted to try it again in another part of Kingsbury Run tonight. Only this time, he'd let the railroad detectives know first what he was going to do.

Are you going with him tonight? I asked Jack. Hell, no, he said. He didn't care if the department fired him, he was never going to get drawn into such a dumb idea again. Besides, this was supposed to be his day off, and he'd already worked nine hours. He wasn't going to work another minute until he got some sleep. He said he was hiding in Tony's, hoping his partner didn't know where to find him.

We drank for another half hour when, all of sudden, Jack ducked down and tried to avoid being seen by the man who had just come into the bar. I knew at once who it must be.

The short, heavy man sauntered over to the table. His suit looked like something I'd expect to find thirty years ago in a rummage sale. He had on a wide cabbage leaf tie with brilliant red and yellow flowers. His black hat with the brim partially down over the right eye was like a movie version of a private detective.

If anything, his physical attributes were a good match for his clothes. Together, they produced an outstandingly unattractive figure. He had a round, beefy face with a long, broad nose, thick lips, and little slit eyes. His hair was almost shaved on the sides, making his large ears stick out all the more.

When Jack introduced me to him, Pete was wearing a broad, almost idiotic, grin. Dennis made a big fuss over his tie, complimenting him profusely on the colors, and winking at Jack and me on the side. Pete was very pleased with the compliment and thanked Dennis. I could sense Jack's partner was not overly gifted intellectually.

Pete was very excited. He had a tip from a prostitute about a guy who cuts the heads off animals to get his kicks. That was just the kind of pervert they were looking for, he told me.

He looked over at Jack and told him they had some work to do. Jack groaned and tried to convince Pete that this lead could wait until tomorrow, but Pete wouldn't hear of it. It had to be tonight.

I told Pete that if Jack wouldn't go with him, I'd be happy to take his place. At first, Pete wasn't particularly warm to the idea, but when Jack continued to refuse, he looked over at me again. I imagine Pete thought that it might not hurt to have someone my size along with him in case there was any trouble.

He made one last effort to convince Jack to go with him, but Jack held his ground. Okay, he told me, you can come along. Dennis winked at me as we got up from the table to leave.

As out of shape as the little fat man was, he walked fast, almost bursting with energy. In a couple of minutes, we were in the police station parking lot where he had parked his car.

He asked me if I knew how to use a gun, and I told him I did. He pulled out a pistol from under the front seat and told me to put it in my pocket. If there was any trouble, I was never to tell anybody the gun was his. I agreed, and we got in the car. Pete said this guy lived just off Cedar around 39th Street. He handed me a scrap of paper with the address and told me to hang onto it.

Then he took off like a bat out of hell. The man drove like a maniac. I commented on it diplomatically, and he laughed. He said he was an ambulance driver years ago before he joined the police force. Now I've seen some ambulance drivers in my time, but never one who drove as recklessly as Pete.

The address was an old apartment building in a sad state of disrepair. I could barely make out the names of the tenants next to the mailboxes. John Derman, the man we came to see, lived on the third floor. The front door to the building wasn't locked, so we walked up the two flights of stairs and knocked on Derman's

THE AMERICAN SWEENEY TODD

door. From the hallway, we could hear loud classical music playing inside. It was Wagner, I think.

Pete banged on the door and told him to open up. The door opened on a chain, and a face peered out. Pete told him it was the police. He repeated the word police in a surprised voice and undid the chain.

The door opened to an enormous mountain of a man. He was at least three inches taller than me and a good seventy pounds heavier. John Derman was about forty-five with a thick head of prematurely gray hair and a mustache to match. He was nicely dressed in a white shirt with the collar open at the top. With his neatly combed hair and horn-rimmed glasses, I thought he looked like a businessman who had just come home from work.

Pete flashed his badge and barged into the apartment. I followed him in and closed the door behind us. The apartment surprised me. It reminded me of a professor's apartment that I had visited when I was in school. While there wasn't a lot of furniture, what there was of it was good quality. On every wall was artwork, mostly framed prints of French Impressionists. There were hundreds of books, neatly shelved in the bookcases that lined several walls.

Pete looked uncouth and out of place in this refined living room, but that didn't bother him at all. He ordered Derman to turn off the music and sit down at the dining room table. Derman did what he was told and sat down at the table in the small dining room that adjoined the living room. Not knowing whether I should sit or stand, I decided to do whatever Pete did. Pete remained standing, pacing around now and then while he talked to Derman. I stood farther back, leaning up against the dining room wall.

Well, he said to Derman accusingly, I hear you're fond of chickens. Derman looked frightened but said nothing. I know all about it, Derman, Pete said, so don't play dumb with me. Why don't you tell me and my pal here what it is you do with chickens.

I had trouble keeping a straight face. I couldn't understand why the police were interested in a guy who had a thing for chickens. In the bar when Pete said the man cut the heads off animals, I had imagined dogs or cats, not poultry.

Derman started to talk. For a man his size, he was remarkably timid and soft spoken. Pete had told me on the way over that Derman was a truck driver, but he must have been mistaken. Derman wasn't like any truck driver I knew.

It's not illegal, he whined. What I do isn't against the law. I don't even kill the chickens. It's the prostitutes who do it. Derman looked like he was going to cry. His bottom lip quivered noticeably.

I don't give two farts in hell if you kill the chickens or not, Pete bellowed at him. I just want to hear about how you do it. I'll decide what's against the law and what isn't.

Derman didn't respond, and Pete was getting angry. Look, pal, he told him, if you don't tell me here, we'll take you down to the station and lock you up for a few days.

No, don't do that, Derman begged. I have to go to work tomorrow. I'll tell you what you want to know. He propped up his head with his elbows resting on the table and started to rub his temples with his fingers. In a low voice, he mumbled his story to us.

Every couple of months, he'd have this real strong urge, and he'd buy some live chickens. He'd take the chickens and a big butcher knife to this whorehouse off Central. They knew him there and were used to doing what he asked. He'd have two prostitutes undress. One of them would rub his penis while the other one beheaded the chickens. Sometimes, he'd have one of the prostitutes rub the knife against his throat, but that was all.

That's not all! Pete roared at him. What about when you have sex with the chickens? I want to know about that.

I couldn't believe my ears. What a weird guy. I tried so hard not to laugh. Fortunately, Pete didn't see the grin on my face. He was so serious. And so was Derman.

Derman turned in his chair to face us. He explained that he couldn't really have sex with the chickens, although he had tried once. He said that its orifice, as he called it, was too small. He'd just have the prostitute hold the chicken while he rubbed his penis between the chicken's wing and its body until he climaxed.

Was that before or after it was beheaded? Pete wanted to know. Derman looked at Pete with pronounced distaste. Before, Derman said firmly, always before. It would be disgusting afterward, he said. Pete agreed somberly.

So you started out with chickens and moved up to humans, Pete said matter-of-factly. Derman looked puzzled. Then Pete took some photographs out of his coat pocket and spread them out on the table in front of Derman. They were morgue photos of the body parts pulled out of the lake and Kingsbury Run.

Our poor chicken lover was horrified by what he saw. He turned them over, unable to look at them any longer. Pete turned them face up again. Come on, he said roughly. It didn't bother you when you cut them up. Why should it bother you now?

Derman gasped. You don't think I did this, he cried, jumping to his feet. Pete pushed him back down in the chair again and told him to stay put.

We've got witnesses who saw you, Pete lied, thrusting one of the pictures in his face. Derman mumbled that wasn't possible. He could never hurt anybody. Then he started to gag. It looked to me like he was going to vomit.

Pete kept at him, though, oblivious to the man's distress. He laid out all the pictures again in front of him on the table. Then it happened and, boy, did it happen. Derman threw up all over the table and the pictures and Pete's coat sleeve. What a stinking mess it was.

I think you ought to let him alone for a few minutes, I suggested to Pete. I went into the kitchen to find some towels for Pete to clean himself off.

Let's get out of here, Pete said in disgust, wiping off his sleeve with the wet towel I gave him. So we left Derman and the pictures and went back out to the car. Pete couldn't stand the smell of his coat, so he took it off and put it in the trunk.

He dropped me off at Tony's and went home. Dennis had already left, but Jack was there drinking with Hanley. I told Jack I really liked his partner, except that I thought he was wasted on the police force. With the right gag writer, he could put Laurel and Hardy out of business.

[Note: No explanation is provided for gap in journal entries between September 1936 and February 1937.]

FEBRUARY 20, 1937

I have been away from this too long. I need it, like medicine, to keep me well. It fills the dark empty space inside me, which stays just beyond the reach of my reason and understanding.

Tonight was almost as good as it has ever been. She was lovely, small, and childlike, like the Lady of the Lake. Her long, silky brown hair smelled so good while I held her to me. Her skin was soft and smooth as I ran my hands over her body.

I don't know what got into me tonight, but I took her twice before it was all over. She got me so excited, I just couldn't get enough. So pliant and yielding, and so very vulnerable.

And at the end, she scarcely made any struggle. She surrendered completely to me. It was just glorious. What a rare and wonderful pleasure. I'm sorry now it has come to an end.

FEBRUARY 21, 1937

I have been particularly cautious tonight, waiting until quite late to take her down to the car. I put her head and arms in a burlap sack with a couple of heavy rocks to keep it at the bottom of the lake. The two pieces of her torso I just threw into the water. At least one of them will float to the surface and wash up on the shore as they have before. The torso will be enough for Dr. Gerber, the new coroner, to tell that I have been busy again.

I hate to do this to Jack just when his goofy partner was starting to leave him alone at night. Sometimes I feel like one of those peddlers on the street corner that sells wind-up toys. He gets the toys all wound up, and they march off in every direction. Ten minutes later, a couple of them have fallen over, and the rest are going slower and slower. Then the peddler winds them all up again, and it starts all over. That's what I'm doing to the police department.

FEBRUARY 27, 1937

Tonight, I got the answer I was looking for. I saw Hanley over at Tony's. After we'd been drinking awhile, I casually mentioned to him that I hadn't seen any more of his stories on the Mad Butcher. He said his editor didn't want anything written on the murder this time. He said that Ness had called the editors of all the newspapers and invited them to lunch the day after the last body was found. He asked the editors not to keep publishing stories about the murders. First, he told them that in order to catch the killer, he needed to have the police free to track down solid clues, not responding to thousands of hysterical calls from everybody with an overactive imagination. The second reason was that the court psychiatrist convinced him that all the publicity was encouraging the murderer to kill again.

God damn that Eliot Ness. I should have known he was responsible for keeping me out of the papers. That sonofabitch wants to hog all the publicity for himself. That's Ness's way of getting back at me for making an ass out of his whole department.

If he can't catch me, and by now he must realize he can't, he wants to convince the city I don't exist. I can hardly believe it. The worst of it is, the newspapers are going along with him. At least for now.

MARCH 1, 1937

I was too depressed yesterday to even get dressed. I stayed in my office and poured whiskey down my throat. Today, I felt a little better and went over to Tony's for some of their heavenly spaghetti.

Hanley was there, sitting with Jack. When I sat down, they were talking about Gerber, the new coroner. There was a rift developing between Ness and Gerber about some report Gerber had put together on the Kingsbury Run murders. The coroner wants the report made public and Ness wants it kept quiet.

I asked Jack and Hanley if either of them had seen the coroner's report. Jack had seen it and started to talk about Gerber's conclusions. I was content to listen and eat at the same time.

First of all, Jack started, we'll have to change the name of the Mad Butcher to the Mad Doctor because Gerber is convinced the killer is a doctor. I was caught so off guard I choked on a piece of meatball. Hanley pounded on my shoulder blades until the piece of meat went down.

Shit. What timing. Nothing like calling attention to myself at a time like that, with a cop and a reporter sitting beside me. When I could talk again, I told them I didn't believe it could be a doctor. I said men become doctors because they want to heal people, not kill them.

Jack agreed with me, but he said the department pays a great deal of attention to what the coroner says. The police were already starting a very thorough investigation of all the doctors living anywhere near the city.

Jack told me not to get upset, but old Pete, his partner, had been asking a lot of questions about me this afternoon. Where was my office? Was I married? That sort of thing. Well, I guess it was bound to happen sooner or later. I have to be very, very careful from now on.

MARCH 2, 1937

Everything Jack said was confirmed in the paper this morning. On page two, there was a small article saying the coroner believed a doctor, frenzied by drugs or alcohol, is the most likely killer, instead of a sex-maddened butcher, which is the police theory. It's a new game now with this Sam Gerber. He's smart enough to realize that a man with medical skill is doing the work. It's an interesting thought, but the police could have been at this very point in the investigation years ago if Gerber had been the coroner then.

It looks as though the police have officially taken notice of me now, almost one month shy of two years after I created the Lady of the Lake. They came to see me late this afternoon. I was treating a patient at the time, so I made them wait for a half hour in the waiting room while I took my good old time with the patient.

There were two of them. I can't recall either of their names, but one of them I recognized from Tony's. He remembered seeing me in there with Dennis and Jack and also knew I was Martin Sweeney's cousin. It doesn't hurt, though, being related to Martin. The cops, particularly the Irish ones, think a lot of Martin.

I invited them into my inner sanctum and fixed them some coffee. I offered them a shot, but they looked at each other and declined. Things must be changing when the cops turn down a shot of whiskey. Probably have Eliot Ness to blame for that.

They had already done some checking around before they came to see me. I wonder if they talked to Mullens himself because they seemed to know every detail of that story. I can just imagine what Mullens told them about me. At any rate, they know I have a temper and a fondness for whiskey. They also know I'm a trained surgeon, which must throw me into the spotlight.

Someone told them I was divorced, too, because they asked a lot of questions about my sex life. I told them I didn't have a sex life. I was still paying dearly for the one I had during those few years of wedded bliss. One of the cops laughed.

The other cop asked me if I ever slept with prostitutes. I told him no and that I never would. I said in my profession, I got a chance to see firsthand what venereal disease did to a person's mind and body. It was a powerful deterrent. Then I launched into a short lecture about the decline of morals in this country. I don't know if they bought that or not. I couldn't tell from their faces.

One of them asked me why I lived in my office instead of getting an apartment. I told him that I was saving all my extra money so I could send my boys to a better school. I pointed to the old picture I have of them on top of my bookcase. Besides, I said, I didn't need anything more comfortable to sleep on than the couch on which they were sitting.

The whole interview didn't take more than forty minutes. At the end of it, they asked me if I ever knew or treated Edward

Andrassy or Florence Polillo. I told them that the names were not familiar to me, but I went through the motions of looking into my medical files.

As they were leaving, the one cop asked me if I had a recent photograph of myself he could borrow for a few days. I told him I didn't, but then he said it didn't matter. He knew where he could get one. I can't think of where he could get a photograph unless it was from someone at the hospital.

I didn't like that at all. I remember there was some guy in that shitty bar where I picked up Flo who said he saw the man she was with that night. But that was in January of last year. I wonder if he could remember me from so many months ago from a photograph. Still, it makes me nervous.

I suppose he could have a photographic memory, but my luck couldn't be that bad. As I recall, the police were going to have some artist work with him to reconstruct the face the guy remembered. If he had a good memory, the police should have had a reasonable likeness of me more than a year ago. Whatever the artist drew back then couldn't have been very good otherwise, someone at Tony's would have said something.

I think the guy in that bar is my only real point of vulnerability. But in the worst case, even if he should identify me as the person talking to Flo that night, it's a long way from proving I killed her. I could just say some fat, old whore came over to my table and bothered me, so I left. Thank God, I left that bar alone. I hope Flo didn't tell anybody there she was going out with me.

I'd better find a new place to hide my journals. I guess if I had any sense at all, I'd burn them today. But I can't bring myself to do it. They're so much a part of me.

What I can do though is clean out one of those steamer trunks with all my junk from medical school and put all but this one volume in it. It has a good sturdy lock on it. I'd better put that doll of Flo's in there too. Then I can take the trunk over to Agnes's house, lock it up, and have her keep it for me.

MARCH 3, 1937

I went to Tony's again tonight. I'm going to have to go there more often until things cool down. It's the only way I can keep in touch with this investigation, now that the newspapers have forsaken me.

Dennis was there with Hanley. Jack was out running around with Pete when I told them about my official visit yesterday. Dennis laughed and said he was glad that they hadn't locked me up yet. He wouldn't have anybody else to buy him drinks and listen to his jokes.

I told them I was a little surprised it wasn't Pete who'd paid me a visit, considering all the questions about me that he'd asked Jack. Dennis explained that a list of doctors had been given to each team of detectives. Pete and Jack had names somewhere near the beginning of the alphabet.

Dennis said Jack had been in earlier tonight to grab a sandwich and a couple of beers. He was out with Pete tonight on a wild goose chase after some colored guy who supposedly has some voodoo charm for transplanting human heads.

Last night Pete dredged up some hermit in Kingsbury Run. Jack said the guy was wearing woolen long johns, two suits, two overcoats, and several hats. When they found him, he was reading scraps of newspaper from the bushel basket of financial clippings he had collected.

Hanley said these police expeditions into the bizarre would make great newspaper stories, if only the editor would publish them. He was a bit discouraged because the paper was still going along with Eliot Ness's request for little or no news coverage. Hanley said he was taking good notes though and when things loosened up, he'd write a series of colorful articles on the investigation.

I left there tonight feeling a little bit safer than I did yesterday. If Dennis or Hanley had heard anything suspicious about me from those other cops that came to visit me, I think I would have sensed that.

JUNE 30, 1937

It looks, from the newspaper this morning, as if Eliot Ness is starting to make himself very unpopular with an important segment of the population. And who better to point that out so publicly than my dear cousin Martin. It gives me such pleasure to see the two of them battle it out in the newspaper.

Yesterday, Ness sent hundreds of cops with tear gas and clubs to break up the labor riots between the AFL and the CIO. The cops made everything worse. Some twenty-five people were hurt.

I can understand why Martin is so upset. First, it leaks out that Ness has an undercover investigation of union leaders underway. And now, he sends in his cops to protect the scabs while they go through the picket line during the strike. Not a popular stand in a blue-collar city like this.

With the strike and the labor riots, it looks like nobody is interested in my work anymore. There was only one small story in each newspaper when they found the bones of some colored whore they think I killed last year. Why the cops think I'd get any pleasure out of killing some nigger whore is beyond me.

It depresses me to live in Eliot Ness's shadow. He can put his foot down on me and virtually stamp out the knowledge that I exist. But, he can't keep the lid on the press forever. Even he doesn't have that much power. I'd love to give him another body to worry about, just when so many people are against him because of what he's trying to do to the unions. But I'm not going to endanger myself in the process.

With what the police already know about me, I must be on their list of star suspects. My temper, my drinking, my surgical ability, and my closeness to Kingsbury Run must be documented somewhere. As dumb as the cops have proven themselves to be, I can't count on that lasting forever. I don't dare get them any more interested in me than they already are.

JULY 1, 1937

What a night this has been. It's almost three o'clock, and I'm too wound up to sleep even though I'm physically exhausted. Much too much activity to fit into such a short space of time. I don't have the same luxury of time I used to.

I feel sure I have completely outsmarted the police once again. The idea came to me Wednesday afternoon. I called the Soldier and Sailors Home in Sandusky and told them I needed to come in for some help with my drinking. I put a note on my office door for my patients to call Driscoll if there were any medical emergencies, then I talked to Driscoll and got things square with him.

I put some whiskey and cigarettes and clothes in my car and drove out to Sandusky. Before I went to the hospital, I pulled off the side of the road and drank almost a third of a bottle. When I got to the admissions officer, he had no trouble believing I was drunk.

So they put me in a room with a couple of other veterans and sent in a doctor to look at me. The treatment consists of an hour of counseling every few days for as long as you can stand to be there.

Generally, I'm free to do whatever I want for most of the day. They don't pay much attention.

I spent the rest of the week relaxing and thinking, talking and playing cards with the other guys. I just marked my time until the weekend.

JULY 3, 1937

Weekends are a real madhouse out there at the VA hospital, especially with the Fourth of July coming up. That's when all the wives and mothers and kiddies come to visit. Nobody noticed this afternoon when I slipped into my car and drove away. When I got to Cleveland, it was almost eight-thirty.

I parked the car on West 25th Street and started to scout around the bars near the West Side Market. I selected this part of town because nobody knows me on the West Side, and I can't afford to make any mistakes this time.

I had talked to several people before I found the right guy. He was by himself and had just come in yesterday from southern Ohio to look for work. He didn't know anybody and slept in a flophouse last night. Around eleven, I told him he could spend the night in my office and save the little money he had. He was real happy to come with me.

When we got back to my office, I parked in the back. As I expected, the building was dark with the exception of the one light they keep on in the first-floor hallway. We went in the back entrance and up to my office.

I tried my best not to rush it. It takes away from my pleasure when I do, but I couldn't help looking at my watch and thinking about everything I still had to do tonight. Damn me for being so compulsive, but time is not on my side anymore.

He was an easy one. Almost as easy as that last whore. Not very big or very strong. He was so relaxed around me. So effusively grateful for my hospitality. I caught him completely off guard.

It was all over around twelve-thirty. I allowed myself fifteen minutes to have a drink and a cigarette before I got to work on him. This time, I planned things a little differently. I threw Dr. Gerber a few curves that I hoped would start to reshape his thinking about the killer being a doctor.

The head I did with my usual finesse. That is my trademark. I wanted Gerber to know it was me and not some copycat. The rest of him I just hacked up like some amateur. The work went much faster when I didn't take my usual care.

Then I did something I haven't done before. I got the idea from reading what the papers published on Jack the Ripper. I cut open his abdomen and chest and took out all his organs, including his heart. That ought to give the papers something to write about.

I quickly wrapped up his body in newspaper and put him in several burlap bags. Then, I put the bags in the trunk of my car and drove down to a deserted part of the Flats, right near the river. Before I dumped him in, I opened the bags up, all except the one with his head. I want him to be found in the next few days while I'm still out in Sandusky.

JULY 9, 1937

My God, I am so glad to be back from Sandusky. I hate living with a bunch of other guys, especially the ones that are a little crazy. I don't know how I ever made it through the war. Of course, there wasn't much choice then. I can only take being around other people for a few hours a day, then I need to have some privacy, some quiet.

Living with those guys twenty-four hours a day, listening to their awful jokes and old stories hour after hour and I start to unravel.

Yesterday I was in a really evil mood. That sniveling little insect in the bed next to me couldn't keep his mouth shut. I warned him to lay off, but he didn't, so I belted him. I really belted him. He went off crying about it to the administration.

I figured it was time to leave. I stayed there long enough to give myself a pretty convincing alibi. The Sandusky papers said they started to find parts of the body in Cleveland on Tuesday. Good thing because I don't think I could have put up with being out there much longer.

When I got back to my office, I went through the Plain Dealer and the Press looking for articles on my latest work. There wasn't anything today in the Plain Dealer and just a small article in the Press. I went down to the basement of the building and found the papers for the past three days.

On Tuesday, the day they found parts of his body, the afternoon paper had the story on the front page. I shared the top headlines with the reopening of the steel mills and the three thousand troops that had been called in to keep peace with the unions. On Wednesday, there was just a small front page article in the morning Plain Dealer, very muted in its tone. The evening Press also had a small article. Yesterday, two days after the body was found, there wasn't a goddamn thing in the Press and only a tiny mention on page four in the Plain Dealer!

I am absolutely amazed that Ness has enough power to suppress the news coverage for three deaths. I could understand how the papers might go along with it last winter with that one prostitute. Then when they found the skeleton of that colored whore, there was almost nothing in the papers about it. Now, another body and there are only a few stories, most of which are very small. I'm so disgusted.

I stopped off at Tony's tonight to have a drink with the guys. Dennis asked where I'd been. I told them that I had to cut back on my boozing and had gone out of town for the "cure."

Jack looked relieved when I told him I'd been away. I'm sure that, by now, those other detectives had talked to him about me. Think how embarrassing it would be for a cop to have one of his drinking buddies be a prime suspect. What a joke. The Mad Butcher drinks a couple of nights a week with the lads from the Third Precinct. Assuming my luck holds out, Jack and Dennis won't ever have to suffer that irony.

I asked Jack how things were progressing on the case. He said the whole department was demoralized about it. He wondered if it would ever be solved. Every lead they had went nowhere.

Dennis thought one day the killings would stop as suddenly as they started, and nobody would ever know who did it or why. That's what happened with Jack the Ripper. Hanley didn't agree. He said the killer was sure to slip up eventually and get caught.

That's what really worries me. I've been so lucky thus far. I can't expect that luck to go on forever, especially since the police have already suspected me. Suppose they figure out what I did in Sandusky. Even if they can't prove it, they could have me followed for the next ten years.

It's time I started looking at this realistically. I've lulled myself into believing that the cops are too stupid to catch me. While that's certainly true of many of the ones I've met, it's not true of all of them. Jack isn't stupid, nor is Dennis. It only takes one smart cop to catch me.

Once the police have a list of suspects, they don't have to be geniuses to follow the suspects until the next killing happens. Then they either have the right list of suspects, or they don't.

I think it's time I put an end to this little adventure while I'm still winning. There's nothing more for me to gain in continuing, and everything to lose. Not that I haven't enjoyed all the attention and the publicity I used to get, not to mention outsmarting the boy hero and his whole police department. But all of that is wearing thin. I'm getting really bored. I don't even get the publicity anymore.

I've got to find some other way of nourishing this big ego of mine. Shit. If I'd put a fraction of the thought and energy into my practice that I have put into making asses out of the police department, I'd be a wealthy man now. I wouldn't have had as much fun, but at least I'd have something tangible to show for my efforts.

Someday when I'm on my deathbed or too old to be prosecuted, I'm going to send my journals to the newspaper. I deserve some recognition for accomplishing what I have. Not only have I committed the perfect crime right under the nose of the nation's greatest crime fighter, but I've done it over and over again.

THE JOURNALS:

EXPECT THE UNEXPECTED

I'm glad that I made the decision to quit. This game has become much too dangerous for me. Those two detectives that came to see me back in March came by again this morning. The police are getting too close.

As I should have expected, they had a whole load of questions about where I was and what I was doing last weekend. They looked a little disappointed that I'd been out of town. I wonder what they would do if I said I'd been here in Cleveland. Well, this was their last chance. If they don't get me this time, there won't be another.

Early this afternoon, Martin called and invited me to dinner this evening at his home. Agnes told him that I was back from my alcohol treatment in Sandusky. I wasn't wild about going over there, but I didn't have much in the way of excuses not to go.

Martin still lives in the old neighborhood. I really love that area with its quiet, shady streets and big, old oak trees. It never changes. It's the same now as it was when I was a kid.

When I went up the walk to the front porch, his daughter Anne ran down to meet me. She threw her arms around me and gave me such a hug. My God, how she's grown. I hadn't seen her since Timmy O'Shea's funeral. Pretty young face with freckles and her mother's features.

Marie seemed really glad to see me. She's always liked me. It's the rogue in me that appeals to her. I'm like her father was, rest his wild soul. I was always surprised that she married someone as straight-laced and sober as Martin when she came from such a fun-loving family. If I had been old enough, I would have married her in a heartbeat. Some spirited combination that would have been.

We went to the back yard where Martin and Mike Jr. were cutting the grass. I grabbed a rake and helped with the clippings. Lord knows how I need the exercise. I love doing little chores like that around other people's homes, but I couldn't stand taking care of the yard when Mary and I were living together.

When we finished, Marie brought us out some iced tea, and we sat there in the backyard. It was so quiet and peaceful there among the hedges and the hydrangea. I felt like I could have sat right in that spot for the rest of my life. The warm sunshine, the sweet fragrance of the rose bushes, it was as though time had stopped.

I can understand exactly why Martin still lives here even though he could afford a much newer and bigger home. It's that quiet continuity with the past. How I envy him his past and his present.

A little while later, Marie and Anne set the picnic table, and we had fried chicken and potato salad. The kids sat with us through the whole meal and then went off to play in the house and the yard. Martin is so lucky to have the family that he does. A wonderful wife and really nice kids. I wish to hell I'd been born with his good fortune.

I asked Martin about the mayoral race. I assumed he decided not to run this year since I had read that someone named McWilliams had the party backing. It didn't seem to bother Martin that he wasn't running. He was contented to campaign like crazy for McWilliams, to bring out the blue-collar vote. He said if McWilliams didn't make it this time, maybe he'd run in the 1939 election. Martin was pretty confident about McWilliams winning since Burton and Ness had made such a mess of the labor situation. When Burton called in the Ohio National Guard with their bayonets and tear gas grenades during the strike, he kissed that blue-collar vote goodbye forever.

After dinner, when Marie was in the kitchen, and it was just Martin and me alone, he asked me how I was really doing. I told him things were fine, but I know he sees through it. After all, for the past few years, I've been living in my office like a hermit with a bottle of whiskey. How great can things be? Especially when he is comparing my life with his own.

He asked me if there was anything at all he could do to help me. Money. Connections. He knows that there is a gulf between us. His hand outstretched is to help pull me over. It's my hand that's not reaching out to him. I'm afraid that there's no going back to the life of Martin and Marie for me. I have gone past the limits of their understanding and forgiveness.

JULY 11, 1937

The weather was so magnificent today I couldn't bear the idea of sitting in my office alone. I called Agnes and asked her if she and Patricia wanted to go for a ride after church. She put together a picnic lunch, and I picked them up around eleven-thirty.

We headed east into Hunting Valley and Chagrin Falls. I followed the Chagrin River Road into the splendid rolling meadows out there, dotted with patches of woods. This lovely spot is where the very wealthy build their country homes and raise their thoroughbred horses. Over the freshly painted white fences, we could see the horses grazing in the sunshine.

Patricia's eyes really lighted up. I don't think she's ever been out there. Lee's not the kind to take his family out for rides in the country. She was thrilled to see the horses, so I pulled off to the side of the road by the river. Across the road, the horses came over to the fence to see us. There was a sleek brown mare and its new foal. I've never seen Patricia so happy as she was when she was feeding some apples to those horses. Kids can be so delighted by such simple pleasures.

While Patricia played with the horses, Agnes and I sat on a blanket by the river's edge. It was the kind of summer day you never want to end. A soft, warm breeze kept it from being too hot. The air out there in the country is so clean and fresh. Such a change from the smoky, sulfurous fumes of the city. I felt completely rejuvenated.

How wonderful it must be to live out there and come home every night to the quiet of the countryside. I could have had a home out there if things had gone differently. A place where my boys would grow up learning to ride horses and where Agnes and Patricia could come for the weekend to get away from their dismal little house.

I'm so fed up with things the way they are now, coming back here night after night to this empty office. I've got to stop living this way. God knows I've got the brains to do anything I want. I just need to discipline myself and not get distracted.

[Note: The remaining entries in this volume are about Dr. Sweeney meeting and setting up an office in suburban Cleveland Heights with Dr. Hurley, a pediatrician. Dr. Sweeney's cousin Martin secured him a position as a medical officer at Cleveland's Wayfarer Lodge for the indigent and homeless. November 21, 1937 is the first entry in this new volume.]

NOVEMBER 21, 1937

Hurley's wife is such a jewel. She's unbelievably aggressive. Everywhere she goes, she takes our business cards and hands them out. And she's involved in everything, the church—they're Protestant

Irish of all things—the PTA, the Eastern Star, Kiwanis. She's done wonders for the new office. There isn't a day that goes by that one of us doesn't get a new patient from something that she's done.

It's a good match, Hurley and me. He takes care of the babies, and I take care of the parents. I told him today that we need to add an obstetrician, then we'd have a full family practice. I was only half serious, but Hurley took me literally and said that he has a friend who might fit the bill. I told Hurley I'd talk to the landlord and see if we could lease more space if his friend is interested.

On my way back to the old office, I happened to go into Wilson's Drug Store today to get some cigarettes. I see that he's hired a new clerk to replace Tommy. She's quite attractive. She's in her mid-twenties, very petite with huge green eyes. I looked to see if she was wearing a wedding ring, but she wasn't. It's unusual for such a pretty girl not to be married at that age.

NOVEMBER 22, 1937

Hurley and I took his wife Elizabeth out to dinner tonight to celebrate. Thanks to her efforts, I had appointments all afternoon and Hurley only had one half hour free. That's a first. It's so good to be making some real money again.

I stopped by Wilson's around eight-thirty to get some more cigarettes, but she wasn't working. Maybe she only works during the day. I'll stop by tomorrow when I go to pick up my shirts from the laundry.

I still need to do some reading tonight. I've got a patient coming in tomorrow with an ulcer that's not responding to treatment. I wish to hell I could find the article I read a couple of weeks ago on that new drug for ulcers. I think that I'm going to have to break down and spend the money to get someone in here a couple of days a week just to answer the phone and get me organized.

NOVEMBER 23, 1937

God, it was really busy here this morning. I thought I was only having three patients come in, but I got two more at the last minute. The flu is really hitting this city hard this year.

I'll just have time to pick up my shirts before I have to be at the Wayfarer's Lodge this afternoon. Jesus, I keep running from place to place. And I still have to stop at Agnes's to drop off the turkey for Thanksgiving dinner. She was kind enough to have my boys over too. I'm very happy about seeing the boys again. They really need me. I just don't know why I let weeks go by without seeing them. My priorities were so screwed up, I didn't even think about them. They reminded me of another one of my failures.

NOVEMBER 29, 1937

I spent the whole morning at the Lodge. It seems like everyone has the flu. It's no wonder, considering what those bums do to their bodies. Even though they can get free food there, most of the time they're too drunk to eat it. And, when they do eat, they wander outside in the freezing cold without coats. One old guy died of exposure last night only two blocks away from the Lodge. He was too boozed up to make it two blocks to a warm bed. What can you do?

This afternoon, I had only four patients at the office here, so I had a chance to go over to the drug store around four-thirty. She was there working. I introduced myself to her and chatted with her until another customer came in. Her name is Jenny Petersen. She's from Millersburg, Ohio, wherever the hell that is. She says it's a little town a few hours southwest of here. It amazes me how I can live in a state for so many years and still not know where anything is.

I asked her if she would have lunch with me tomorrow. She looked very embarrassed, but she said yes. She appears to be very shy, but I think she likes me. She's even prettier than I remembered, especially when she smiles. Her big eyes are so expressive. She almost talks with her eyes.

I've got to remember to wear my new suit tomorrow. Women are always impressed with a man who dresses well. Jesus, it's been so long since I've taken a woman out. I'm not sure I know how to act anymore. I don't know what they expect nowadays.

I've still got another several hours of work to do before I can hit the sack. I almost forgot that Hurley's wife has me speaking tomorrow night on diabetes to her Eastern Star chapter. I wish now that I'd put it off to next month. But, I shouldn't complain. It's things like this that bring me new patients. New patients mean more money. More money means I can stop living in my old office.

NOVEMBER 30, 1937

I'm so tired I can hardly write. I had back-to-back patients here this morning. I just made it out of here for my lunch with Jenny. It was a good thing she only had an hour because I had to race on over to the other office for a whole afternoon of work. Then we had a kid brought in at the end of the day with an awful fracture in his arm. After that, there was the Eastern Star meeting and the coffee hour.

The highlight of the day was lunch. We walked over to Francine's, which is one of the quietest places around here. Jenny looked beautiful in a green dress that almost matched her eyes. I could see the heads turn as I walked down the street with her.

She said she's twenty-eight, but she looks several years younger. She and her husband are separated. Fairly recently, I gather. I could see it was a touchy subject, so I didn't probe. I asked her if she had any kids. She hesitated and said no. I thought I detected pain in her eyes when she said that, so I didn't push it any further.

She's only been in Cleveland for a few weeks. Her whole life has been spent in Millersburg. Her father's a dairy farmer and a bit of a religious fanatic, from what I gather. Her family is Danish. She said she didn't learn to speak English until she went to school. I noticed she still has a slight trace of an accent.

She's more of a listener than a talker. Most of the time, I was doing the talking. Not because I planned to, but because she asked me so much about myself and my work. She is awed by me being a doctor.

I asked her to dinner on Friday. I would have loved to make it sooner, but things have become so hectic that I didn't see how I could fit in a leisurely evening until the weekend. Maybe I can get tickets to something at the Playhouse or Severance Hall. No, I'll wait on that. She doesn't strike me as the intellectual type.

DECEMBER 4, 1937

Thank God I was able to sleep late this morning. I didn't realize how exhausted I was. Not that we were out late last night. I was back here before eleven. It's just the whole week of working such late hours and running back and forth from one place to the other really takes its toll.

Last night was very pleasant. I took Jenny over to that Hungarian restaurant on Buckeye where they have a gypsy violinist. It's very romantic. Women seem to like dark restaurants with flickering candles. Me, I like to see what I'm eating.

Jenny was a lot more talkative last night than she was when we had lunch together. Her shyness has almost completely disappeared, and she was pretty open about the hard life she's had. The guy she married was part of the Danish community she lived in and had a small farm not too far from her father's. She said that he drank quite a lot and that the liquor would bring out a crazy violent streak in him. How familiar that all sounds. The Danes must be like the Irish.

I asked her if his violence was the reason they separated. She became very serious and said that something had happened which made it impossible for her to live with him. I didn't push it any further. There was a silence as she decided whether to confide in me. Finally, she told me the whole story.

One day when she was six months pregnant, her husband had been drinking heavily and got some notion in his head that she was unfaithful to him. He beat her badly. She went into labor, and the baby died. What a hell of a thing to happen. They ought to string that bastard up.

She said her father threw a fit when she told him she wanted to get a divorce. He gave her a lot of religious malarkey and told her she must learn to live with her husband's weaknesses. I can't understand how a parent can let a lot of religious bullshit doom his child to a life of misery. The responsible thing to do would have been to help her get out of that marriage.

I give her credit for leaving there and coming to a strange city all by herself. That takes some courage. She said she can't let her parents know where she is because her father will tell her husband, who will come after her.

I tried to set her mind at ease by reminding her Cleveland is a very big city, and it's easy to disappear. She was smart enough to take the precaution of going by her mother's maiden name, so she shouldn't have too much to worry about. For someone with so little real world experience, she is remarkably sophisticated.

There's something about her that stirs up all the old desires in me. Feelings I thought were dead forever. I wanted to take her tiny body, press it up against mine, and protect it from all the things that frighten her.

She's so different from Mary. Even before we were married, Mary expected things from me. She'd pout if I didn't do just what she wanted. Mary thought she was really something back then. I guess, maybe she was. She was thin and pretty with long, curly hair and big, opulent breasts.

But Mary wasn't any prettier than Jenny. It's just that Mary knew she was attractive and manipulated people with her looks. Jenny isn't like that at all. Jenny is so delighted at the smallest courtesy. I can't imagine a gentle woman like Jenny ever turning into a bitch like Mary.

In retrospect, I think Mary enslaved me with her body. I couldn't keep my hands off her, and she knew it. I was so inexperienced with women when I met her. The few women I'd known before her never let me do the things Mary did. Mary knew she needed to use her body to catch a husband, and that's exactly what she did. Not much chance of that happening with Jenny. She has the body of a twelve-year-old.

DECEMBER 22, 1937

I left the Heights office a little early today, so I'd have more time to be with her. I guess I wanted to ask her to spend Christmas with me too.

But she declined. I'm not really sure why. I thought, at first, she was thinking of going back to Millersburg to see her parents, but she said she didn't dare. She was afraid if she went back she'd have to stay.

When she told me she couldn't afford to take time off work, I offered to give her some money, but she wouldn't accept it.

Apparently, she's going to stay by herself here in the city. She said Christmas was always a very special religious holiday for her, and she was planning to go to the Lutheran church services on Christmas Eve.

After work, she came over to the office about five with a big box of Christmas cookies she baked for me to take to the men at the Lodge tomorrow. She said she had a devil of a time convincing her grouchy old landlady to let her use the kitchen, but in the end, the old lady was happy enough to eat a whole batch of Jenny's cookies on her own. Jenny says Christmas isn't Christmas without cookies. It was the least she could do to make the homeless men at the Lodge feel happy during the holidays. Just as well that I'm taking in the cookies because if she saw what a bunch of drunken bums they were, she might feel less charitable.

When she got to the office, I was struggling to wrap all the gifts I have for the boys. She took pity on my miserable efforts and did all the wrappings for me. She finished in an hour and a half what would have taken me three hours at least. And what a difference in the end result!

She's such a genuinely good person. I wish I had met someone like her years ago.

I wanted tonight to be our Christmas dinner together, so I made reservations at the Hollenden House for seven-thirty. Just as we were being seated, I saw Eliot Ness and his wife sitting several tables away. I noticed his eyes following Jenny appreciatively as she walked to the table. It gave me a distinct pleasure to see how much more attractive Jenny is than his wife.

He was seated so that I had a clear view of his face. He didn't look very happy, nor did his wife. He seemed to have aged quite a bit from the boyish face I remembered from a couple of years ago.

THE AMERICAN SWEENEY TODD

He was hitting the booze hard. I counted five drinks just in the two and a half hours or so we were having dinner. It's difficult for me to believe I had once considered him to be so important. Thank God, I've come to my senses. I think I have finally got my head on straight now.

Ness kept looking over at Jenny. She seemed very flattered at the attention and asked me if I knew him. I told her who he was and that I only knew him by reputation. He was not high on the list of people I wanted to know well.

After dinner, I gave Jenny the Christmas present I bought for her. It was a gold bracelet I picked up at a real nice jewelry store in Shaker Heights. She was thrilled with it. She had never had a real gold bracelet before. It looked very attractive on her, accentuating her tiny wrists and hands.

She had a gift for me too. A white wool scarf. I can't imagine how she could afford it. It's very handsome, but I wish she wouldn't spend so much on me when she makes so little.

It was as nice a Christmas dinner as I have ever had. One of the very few I was sober enough to remember. I felt comfortable with her and wanted very much for our relationship to get closer. I was slowly overcoming my fear of touching her. On the way out of the restaurant, I reached out to hold her hand. She seemed to like that.

When we got to her rooming house, I walked her, as I always did, up to the door. She looked so beautiful standing in the light with a few tiny snowflakes falling on her hair. I said I hoped she would have a good Christmas and took her hand up to my lips and kissed it. I wish I could be with you, I told her.

Her lips were parted in a slight smile. I put my arms around her shoulders very lightly and kissed her on the forehead. She moved closer to me, giving me the courage to draw her up to me and kiss her on the lips. I know it sounds crazy, considering the number of times we've been together, but I had never kissed her before. I've wanted to, but the timing never seemed right. For all my blarney, I guess I really am shy with women.

DECEMBER 30, 1937

I took the boys out to eat at a restaurant. And then, Richard Donnelley, my friend from medical school, was nice enough to invite the boys and me over to his home for dinner next week. He has a boy just about Frankie's age. It will be good to see old Richard again.

I called Jenny at work as soon as I got back from dinner with the boys. Jesus Christ, I couldn't get her out of my mind, but I didn't tell her that. I was able to stop for a few minutes to see her at the drugstore. She was as beautiful as ever. Just looking at her gets me aroused. I can't wait to be with her again.

I had hoped to get together with her, but we had an emergency down at the Lodge, and I got stuck there until almost nine o'clock. Goddamn it. Now, the first chance I'll have to see her is tomorrow night. That reminds me, I still haven't made any reservations. I hope it's not too late to go somewhere nice.

JANUARY 1, 1938

I think last night was the first New Year's Eve I have every truly enjoyed. No wild parties. No frenetic merriment. Instead, a quiet, elegant dinner and dancing at the Cleveland Hotel with my wonderful companion.

She looked just lovely tonight in a long, light-yellow gown, wearing the bracelet I gave her. Next year, I'm going to get her the necklace to match.

This was the first time I'd ever seen her hair fixed in an upsweep. It makes her look totally different than when she wears it down around her shoulders. So classy and sophisticated. I was really proud to be seen with her.

But the dinner and dancing weren't the highlights of the evening. It was afterward. The dancing and the champagne brought us together physically much more than we had been before. I think both our inhibitions were slipping fast as we danced so close.

Still, I had enough presence about me not to overstep my boundaries. Around one o'clock, I asked her if she wanted me to take her home. She giggled and suggested that we go back to my office for a nightcap. I can't do justice to the description of how I was affected by that suggestion. My mind reeled with the possibilities.

Back at my office, I fixed our drinks, and she sat close to me on the couch. She was very affectionate and very tipsy. I let her initiate things and then I'd cautiously press forward. I wasn't sure how far she'd let me go. I didn't want to risk ending the evening by being too aggressive.

It was perfect, though, the way it unfolded. Each new intimacy stoked my desire. Every unchecked advance was a wonderful gift. Finally, I knew she would let me have her completely. I was determined this would be our finest hour, and I took her as gently and passionately as I've ever taken a woman.

God, how I wish she would have stayed the night. Once was not nearly enough to satisfy me. But she wanted to get back to her rooming house so there would be no raised eyebrows from her landlady in the morning.

I'm starting this new year with more optimism than I have had since I graduated medical school. I feel once again that I can and will be successful—not only in my work but in my personal life. I look forward to having my boys with me again, and maybe, just maybe, if I am very lucky, a new wife.

I had a devil of a time sleeping last night. Too much champagne. Wine always does that to me. It makes me tired, but then it wakes me up several hours later, and I can't get back to sleep.

Jenny spent the afternoon here at my office. The weather was too bad to do anything but stay indoors. She must have liked our lovemaking last night because she was anxious to do it again and again. In fact, when the afternoon was over, she had completely exhausted me. She has a very strong sex drive, I'm happy to say. I wonder if it would continue when we got married or whether she'd go cold on me like Mary did.

Jenny makes me feel like I'm handsome and very desirable. Mary made me think I was lucky to be going out with her. Jenny, on the other hand, makes me feel like she really wants to have me.

The weather cleared up enough around six, so we brushed the snow off the car and drove out to a restaurant. We found a small place down Broadway that served nice hot roast beef sandwiches and mashed potatoes. Both of us were so tired that I took her home after we had dinner. Hopefully, I'll be able to get some sleep tonight.

JANUARY 2, 1938

I'm still having a lot of trouble sleeping. I've decided it's because I'm so keyed up. Not only with all this work, which has been quite a change of pace from the past couple of years, but the emotions that are new in my life. It would be silly not to think all this change in such a short period of time wouldn't disrupt my equilibrium somewhat.

I stopped by to see Agnes this morning and checked the incision. She seems to be recovering very well from her gallbladder operation. Driscoll did a good job on her, as I knew he would. She's picked up a bad cold, though, which has settled in her chest. Every time she coughs, the incision hurts. I brought her some strong cough medicine. That's about all I can do for her. I told her I'd stop by Monday night and listen to her chest. I want to make sure there aren't any complications, given her weakened condition.

I was thinking of telling Agnes about Jenny, but I didn't just yet. I'll wait until Agnes is better and then have them meet face to face. I sure hope they like each other. I took Jenny to the art museum this afternoon as I promised her I would. I was right in my initial assessment. She's not very well educated, but she has an open mind. I enjoyed teaching her the little bit I knew about the paintings we saw.

We went to dinner at a tiny Italian restaurant on Murray Hill. I particularly like those small, intimate restaurants, but the spaghetti wasn't nearly as good as Tony's.

What a day I've got in store for me tomorrow. I have to be down at the Lodge at seven-thirty in the morning and back here at ten and then at the Heights office at one. Hurley says his wife has appointments booked for me through six-thirty.

[Note: There are no entries in this volume from early January 1938 to March 15, 1938.]

MARCH 15, 1938

I am so tired. I barely slept at all last night. I've been having the worst dreams lately. They're so bad they wake me up and then I can't get back to sleep. I think it might be the barbital that's doing it. Maybe I'll try something else.

The only good part of my day was when I drove Jenny downtown at lunchtime so she could apply for a job at Higbee's. The employment office was very encouraging about her prospects, but they said it would take three weeks for her to get an answer. It's a lot better wage than Wilson pays her, and there are some chances for advancement. Of course, if my plans work out properly, she won't need to have a job at all.

I tried to do my accounts this evening. Hurley's wife does them for the other office, and I pay her something every week for that, but I still have to keep the accounts for this office here. I'm months behind. If I wasn't so disorganized with all my receipts, I could probably hand it all over to a bookkeeper. But, as it is now, I almost have to do it all myself. I think I'm going to put it off for one more day. I can't keep my mind focused on it.

I'm so restless. I keep fighting this desire to go out to the bars for a few hours. There's something in me that needs a little bit of sleaze. Like a vitamin or a mineral, of which I need just a trace. Otherwise my mind doesn't function properly.

MARCH 16, 1938

I had lunch with Martin today. I suggested we go someplace nice like the new Stouffer's restaurant, but he just about had a fit when I mentioned that place. He started ranting about how the Stouffer brothers conspired with Eliot Ness and the mayor to destroy the entire union movement in the city. I didn't know what the hell he was talking about, so I offered to meet him at the City Grill.

I don't think I've ever seen Martin so wound up. I've been so busy these past months that I haven't paid any attention to city politics, and I completely stopped following the adventures of Eliot Ness last fall.

What's got Martin so riled up is this labor scandal Ness uncovered. I guess I have seen a few headlines about it, but I didn't read the stories. Martin said Ness and Burton had a deal with the big business owners in town to try to break the unions. When they failed to bust up the unions during the strike last summer, Martin said Ness planned to discredit the unions by putting some of the union leaders in jail.

Vernon Stouffer and his brother went to Eliot Ness and claimed the leaders of two construction unions tried to extort money from them to have the new restaurant finished on time. For that and other extortion attempts, Ness sent the two union leaders to the Ohio penitentiary earlier this month.

I asked Martin if the union leaders were guilty. He looked a little sheepish and said, of course, they were guilty, but that wasn't the point. Ness was out to discredit the whole labor movement. I listened politely to another ten minutes of impassioned rhetoric and then I switched the subject to my main reason for inviting him to lunch.

I told him I was going to have to resign my position at the Wayfarer's Lodge. I wanted him to know first since he had gotten the position for me. I explained I couldn't spare the time, along with my two offices. In fact, I told him that probably next year, I'd close the office on Broadway and just work out of the Cleveland Heights office. The business in the new office was growing much faster than I ever had expected.

Martin was really happy things were going so well for me in my practice. He asked me how I was doing with my personal life. I don't know why, but I spilled out all my plans to him. Everything I wanted to do with the boys, a house, and even Jenny.

Martin said he suspected as much when I called him up for advice about Jenny's divorce situation. I asked him to keep quiet about it for the time being because I hadn't said anything to Agnes about Jenny. I told Martin I wanted to be very sure about the relationship before I went introducing her to my family.

Martin understood. He told me he looked forward to meeting Jenny, especially if she was as pretty as I told him she was. He said he wanted so much for me and the boys to have a good life together.

I went away from lunch feeling good. I like Martin. He's so genuine. No bullshit. I feel so much closer to him now than I ever did before.

Before I get too tight tonight, I've got to write my resignation letter. I want to get it to the Lodge tomorrow morning. I'll give them two weeks' notice and extend it a third week if they're really in a bind. Resigning that post takes a load off my shoulders. I can make twice as much at the new office in the same amount of time. Plus, I don't have to run around as much.

I'm going to have to cut back my hours. Sometimes I feel like I'm falling apart. I'm starting to fly off the handle every time some little thing goes wrong. I nearly bit the head off the new receptionist when she screwed up on the appointments for Monday afternoon.

Maybe once I get rid of this other job at the Lodge, I can cut back on the barbital too. I'm really asking for trouble taking that stuff with as much whiskey as I drink. It's just that I need it to calm my nerves. Nothing else seems to work as well.

Sometimes, I wonder if the barbital is doing something to my mind. About a month after I started taking it, I started having those fantasies again. It's either the drug or I'm losing my mind. Maybe I'll lay off the barbital for a few days and see if it makes any difference. Who am I kidding? That stuff is so addictive. I'd end up in the hospital if I didn't keep taking it every day.

Maybe I should see a psychiatrist. It's just that I don't have any confidence they can really help me. They're such witch doctors. I'm not sure they've ever cured anybody. I couldn't ever completely open up to one anyway. It'd be too dangerous to tell him what I've done. I don't think they can help a person unless they know everything.

I'm glad I went out tonight. It helped me take the edge off my nerves. The one good thing about these low life bars is that I never have to watch what I say or do. I can be completely relaxed without any regard to the social implications.

The minute I walk into those places, I am immediately the most successful person in the whole place. And these people look at a doctor as someone right below the pope in their scheme of things. I suppose it's kind of an ego boost to be so exalted, if even among the lowly.

I need to pull away from those bars when I have to. Last night, I came home just before midnight. Things were starting to get a little out of hand, but I didn't do anything I'd regret. I made sure I didn't have more than one whiskey every hour, which seems to keep the beast in chains.

I've just been working too hard. Once I ease up, things will get better. They've got to get better, or I'll end up in the loony bin like my old man.

I almost lost track of a very important occasion. Tomorrow is St. Patrick's Day. If Jenny's cold is better, we can go over to Dugan's and start out there. I'd like to introduce her to my friends. Even if she's not feeling well enough to go with me, I'll go there by myself. I can't get into too much trouble at Dugan's.

MARCH 17, 1938

And a happy St. Paddy's Day to you too!!! Good night and good morning.

MARCH 18, 1938

I looked at what I wrote last night and marvel that I could write anything at all. The day after St. Paddy's should be a holiday just like New Year's Day so people can sleep it off. It's too cruel to have to work with such a vicious hangover.

At lunchtime, I called Jenny to see how she was feeling. She still sounds all congested. I told her to keep taking what I had prescribed for her a few days ago. When it starts moving down into her chest, I'll put her on something else.

I fibbed a bit and told her I had a lousy time last night. I said I went to Dugan's for a couple of hours and came back here to bed. She wouldn't have enjoyed last night anyway, even if she didn't have a cold. She hates it when I drink a lot, and she doesn't like to be around other people who are drinking heavily. Needless to say, everyone at Dugan's, including myself, was totally shit-faced the whole night. There was no point in telling her that. What she doesn't know won't hurt her.

There was a pair of lacy white panties on the back seat of my car when I stumbled into it this morning. I must have had a really good time last night. It's a damn good thing I found those panties before Jenny did. I'd never be able to come up with a good explanation. Something so stupid and trivial could destroy our whole relationship.

After I nap for a couple of hours, I'm going out for the hair of the dog. I need some other distraction to take my mind off my work. A tiny dose of sin before I see Jenny tomorrow night.

MARCH 19, 1938

We went out to eat tonight at a new restaurant that opened up at Shaker Square. The food wasn't bad, but the prices were outrageous. Afterward, we went back to my office. Jenny wanted to make love. It wasn't one of my finest performances. I didn't seem to be in the mood.

I don't know what's the matter with me. There must be something constitutionally wrong. Here I have a beautiful, passionate woman like Jenny, and all I think about is that whore I had last night.

Worse than that is what I really wanted to do to the whore and didn't. It took every ounce of self-control I had not to give into my real desires. Maybe I need a priest instead of a psychiatrist. There's something evil inside me begging to get loose. God forbid it does.

Jenny can see something is wrong. How nervous I am. I've tried to downplay it to her, blaming it on overwork. I don't want her to think I'm falling apart. Jesus Christ, I could lose her. The last thing she is going to do is get tied down to another man who has a bunch of problems.

I took her home a little after midnight tonight. At the door, I held her for the longest time. I wish now I'd begged her to stay the night.

She suggested we don't get together tomorrow afternoon. That maybe I should rest. No, I need to be with her. I didn't tell her that sometimes I'm afraid to be alone.

Right after I saw her to the door, the need came over me with an awful intensity. I wanted to go to the bars again. To feel the excitement of the hunt. My mind started to rationalize me in that direction, but I fought it down and came back here to the office.

I took a lot of barbital to knock me out. I feel like a wild animal that needs to be tranquilized and then locked up in a cage for the night. Sometimes I wish they would just come and put a bullet through my head.

MARCH 20, 1938

I went over to see Agnes for about an hour after she got back from church. I still haven't said anything to her about Jenny. I don't know why I keep putting that conversation off. It's crazy, but it's almost as if I expect Agnes to be jealous of any relationship I have with anybody else. Maybe, I'm afraid Agnes might not like her. That I might be faced with a choice between her and Jenny. I certainly don't need any pressure like that on me now.

This afternoon, Jenny and I went to a Cary Grant movie. I slept through most of it, but she seemed to like it. Afterward, we went to a restaurant on Buckeye. The food was Hungarian and really excellent. I've never had better cherry strudel.

After dinner, we went back to my office and listened to the radio. She loves to look through my medical books. While she looked at the books, I threw together some information for that talk I have to give tomorrow night to the parents at Cleveland Heights High School. Another one of Hurley's wife's command performances.

It was so good having Jenny there while I worked. She helps me stay focused on what I should be doing. I'm afraid if she hadn't been there, I would have found myself in the bars downtown. I hope I can hang onto her while I get these problems of mine under control once and for all. I took her home around eleven and came back here to bed.

MARCH 21, 1938

I was buried in work today. Then I had this affair at the high school until nine. After it was over, the need came over me again. I called up Jenny's rooming house, looking for her and hoping I could stop by and take her out for some coffee somewhere. Just to be with her and not be alone. But the landlady said she wasn't there. I can't imagine where she would be after nine at night.

My mind is my worst enemy. It crafts such innocent rationalizations for doing anything it wants. Then when I give into it, one thing leads to another, and pretty soon everything is out of control.

My mind told me I needed to unwind. That I should stop off at a bar and have a few drinks. Talk to some people. Relax before I came back and went to bed. But I can't trust myself anymore. I never know how the evening will end up. I was able to fight it down, but I have no confidence I'll always be strong enough to resist the temptation.

I can't let myself throw away everything I've been working for all these months. It's all within my grasp now. Jenny. The boys. A home for the first time in my life. Respect in the community. There's nothing more I need.

MARCH 22, 1938

I felt very fragile today, so I called up Jenny and told her I needed to see her after work. I told her I had tried to see her last night, but her landlady said she was out. I didn't want Jenny to feel like she had to account to me for every hour of her day, but I was a little curious about what she was doing so late last night. I should have known it was perfectly innocent. She said she was talking to a woman who also rented a room in the same house. The woman had just moved in, and they were getting to know each other over a cup of coffee in the woman's room. Jenny explained that the landlady didn't realize she was down the hall when I called.

Jenny came over to the office with a big bag of rock candy, which she knows is my favorite. God bless that woman. She's the best thing in my life.

I think she wanted to make love, but I wasn't able to emotionally. I've got all this frightening garbage in my head. Sometimes it makes it very hard for me to carry on a normal relationship. She stayed until a little after eleven. When she kept yawning, I took her home.

The need never seems to go away. All I can do is try to suppress it, stay in my office, and attempt to drown it in whiskey and barbital.

MARCH 23, 1938

After work, I was very restless. In fact, I was restless the whole afternoon. I just couldn't keep my mind on my patients. I even called one woman I know very well by the wrong name. I tried to call Jenny, but she wasn't home from work yet. Then I tried the drug store, but she'd already left. I imagine she went shopping or something. I've got to stop clinging to her when I feel so restless. She's going to think I'm crazy.

I can't go on living like this. Always afraid of going alone to bars. Worrying about what's going to happen at the end of the evening. I decided tonight to confront it and deal with it head on.

I started out at Dugan's. There's no way I can get into any trouble at Dugan's. Patty's getting married next month. Her dad is real proud of her for landing the guy she's marrying. He's a foreman for American Steel and Wire and probably brings home a pretty good paycheck. I'm going to miss her, though. She says her future husband won't let her work at the bar even under her father's watchful eye. Just as well. She should have children. She's almost twenty-seven.

After a couple of hours, I went to Tony's. Jack and Dennis were there, but Hanley had to work late to finish up some story for tomorrow's paper. They asked where I'd been. They missed my company. I whispered that I had a girlfriend who was taking up all my time in the evenings.

I indulged myself in a plate of their terrific spaghetti. It never changes. I love that thick, dark-red sauce with those wonderful, big meatballs. I have no doubt that if I ate here every night, I'd gain back all the weight I've lost in the past several months.

I asked Jack how things were going on his favorite case. He said they hit a dead end months ago. Not that it stopped his goofy partner Pete from checking out every screwball and stumblebum. It's been so many months now with no new bodies, the police are wondering if the killer has moved somewhere else.

Maybe one of his prospective victims killed him, I suggested. Jack said he didn't think they'd ever know. He was just as happy working on other cases. Ones he felt he had a fighting chance of solving.

Dennis wanted to know about my new girlfriend. I told the two of them I was planning to get married. Instead of congratulating me, both of those bums tried to talk me out of it. They really did. Dennis, poor lad, because he's so unhappily married to a shrew. And Jack, because he's a guy who's going to hang onto his bachelorhood as long as his handsome Irish face will let him. He said he had a new girlfriend too. The previous one tried to give him an ultimatum about getting married, so he dumped her and found someone else.

I defended my decision. I explained the situation with my boys. How I had to get them away from my ex-wife. I told them I'd found a very special woman. Pretty, smart, very passionate. I think I was eloquent enough to make my point. At least they stopped giving me a hard time.

I only stayed an hour and a half. Those two guys are very tedious when they've had too much beer and get bogged down in trivial police department politics. I was itching to go downtown to the bars on Prospect, where the music is loud, and the company uninhibited. My soul, God save it, is in the dives on Prospect with the whores and the penny con men.

There are a lot of bars in that area. I know them all like the back of my hand. I drifted from one to another, no more than two drinks at each place. Enjoying myself, talking to the people there. Some of them I have talked to before. Others are new.

I feel some kind of link with these people. A link that defies logic. I'm comfortable with them. At home with them, even though they are so remote from me socially and intellectually. I've stopped trying to understand it and just accept it as fact.

In past years, when this was my prime hunting ground, I was as at home here as all the other hunters and their prey. It is the law of nature in these downtown bars, no different than in the jungle. The hunter has his needs. He satisfies his needs. It's all over quickly and quietly, and life goes on as if nothing had happened. A perfectly natural system.

I got back here before twelve-thirty. The itch has been scratched with no nasty consequences. Perhaps I have been selling myself short on the subject of self-control.

MARCH 24, 1938

Goddamn my arrogance! I've got to get some help, and I've got to get away from here. I can't count forever on whatever patron saint bailed me out tonight. I thought I was in control. What a goddamn joke I have played on myself. God only knows who or what is really in control of me.

I went out again tonight believing I would be all right. The change didn't happen right away. It's very gradual over a period of hours and drinks. It's like my will is slowly dissolving. I become a different person. No, I become a different being, one who controls me. My whole mind and body exist only to satisfy its driving lust.

It's not a mindless beast that attacks the closest victim. No, it hunts. It selects its prey, choosing the one who will bring the most pleasure and the least danger. It surveys its choices, selects a victim, talks to the victim, and rejects the victim. It starts again. It goes on until the best one is found, even if it takes all night.

A perfect one was chosen. No one to miss him. No children or wife to suffer from his loss. I brought him here, fed him, and gave him some whiskey to drink. He relaxed, and I waited for the opportunity. Then came the knock on the door.

A perfunctory knock at best because he always comes in right after he knocks. It was Louie. He looked at me and my companion and apologized for disturbing us so late. The furnace had broken down, and he wanted to warn me to bundle up tonight. And then he wanted me to keep the faucets running a little so that the pipes wouldn't freeze.

How timely his visit. Not only did he save the life of the miserable creature who ate at my table, but he saved me from the black emptiness which resides at my very core. It was an omen. I must get help.

MARCH 25, 1938

I was just barely able to function today. I didn't sleep at all last night. At work, my nerves were so shot I had to keep taking barbital just to keep from shaking apart.

I called into the Heights office and had my appointments rescheduled for next week. I explained to Hurley I was going out of town on family business, and I wasn't sure exactly what day I'd be back. He can see how frayed my nerves are. He knows something's wrong. I let him think I'm having problems with my ex-wife and the kids.

That's the story I'm going to tell Jenny, too, when I call her. I hate like hell to leave her, but I've got to get help quickly, and the only place I know is the veterans hospital in Sandusky. I wish I could take her with me. She is so central to my future. I feel so calm around her. Sometimes I wish I could tell her all about myself. Open up my innermost secrets. But I don't dare tell her any of that. She would run out of here screaming.

I stopped over at Agnes's. She was alone. Lee was still at work, and Patricia was up in her bedroom doing homework. Agnes knew there was something wrong the minute she saw me. Sometimes I think she comes very close to reading my mind.

For the first time that I can remember, she offered me whiskey instead of coffee. She said I looked like I needed a drink. She poured one for herself, too, as though she were preparing herself for bad news.

We sat at the kitchen table. There was no small talk. She expected me to get to the crux of what was troubling me, and I did. That is, within the limits of what I can say to her. I told her I was having some very severe emotional problems which required professional help, and I was going to look for that help in Sandusky.

She listened quietly and then she asked me something very intuitive. She said, Frank, what have you done? When I think about that question, it was really unexpected. I would have expected she'd have asked me about my drinking or the pressures of my work. I didn't quite know how to answer such a direct question. I don't like to lie to Agnes, yet I cannot tell her the whole truth.

I told her I couldn't tell her what I'd done. I was too ashamed. She put her hand on the top of mine and looked me straight in the eye. All she said was, I love you, Frank. No matter what you've done, I love you. I believe that even if Agnes had looked down into the black core of my soul, she would still love me. I hope I will never have to test that belief.

It's almost six-thirty now. If I had any sense at all, I'd drive out tomorrow morning. It's just that I don't trust myself being here tonight, not after what almost happened yesterday. I'll give Jenny a call, pack up a few clothes, and hit the road before I change my mind.

Jenny. I don't know what to do about her. I feel like she is slipping away from me, and I'm powerless to stop it. I can't put my finger on it, but there's something in her voice that's different. It seems more distant now. God, I hope I'm just imagining this. I'm under so much pressure.

MARCH 29, 1938

God help me. I don't know if there is anyone else who can. I talked with the psychiatrist for a while. It was the first time I'd spent any time with him. What a fucking incompetent! Goddamn, worthless Army doctors! I told him I wanted to stay knocked out for the whole weekend. Jesus, I even had to tell him what to prescribe. He did what I told him to do, and I stayed in a stupor for two days straight.

When I woke up yesterday in the late morning, I knew I was not in control anymore. The psychiatrist was nowhere around and nothing was prescribed for me except for the barbital which I needed to keep functioning.

I knew perfectly well what was going to happen, and I was powerless to stop it. My will power had been paralyzed. About eleven o'clock, I got dressed and went into town and found a liquor store. I bought a couple of bottles. My body was screaming for a drink. I took a few gulps of whiskey, lighted a cigarette, and went looking for a hardware store. Pretty soon I found one and bought everything I needed. The knife. The spade. Some burlap. I put the things into the trunk of the car and drove around the town and a few miles outside. I found a wooded spot a few miles south of Sandusky which would serve very well for that night.

I went back to the hospital in the early afternoon. Drinking and pacing around as I waited impatiently for the evening. I indulged myself in all my familiar fantasies. It is a ritual I go through before the hunt begins.

By five o'clock, I couldn't wait any longer. I left the hospital and drove into Sandusky. It didn't take long to find the kind of places I was looking for. I searched several of the bars before I had any luck. Then I found him. He was a drifter who had hitched his way into town from Flint, Michigan. He was pretty drunk when I found him, so I didn't have to spend much to get him into the state I wanted him.

On the pretense of giving him a place to sleep, I got him to come with me in the car. He was so drunk that he passed out while I drove out of town. God, I was so excited as I drove, I could hardly stay on the road. What I wanted to do was just to pull off on the side of the road and get it over with. But I restrained myself and headed out to the place I'd found that afternoon.

I parked the car on a deserted stretch of dirt road. He was still out cold. I took off my suit jacket and shirt and put them in the back seat. Then I put on the orderly's smock I took from the hospital this evening, picked up the knife, and walked around to the passenger side of the car.

He opened his eyes briefly, gave me a very confused look, and passed out again. There was no way he was going to walk on his own, so I hoisted him up over my shoulder and carried him to a spot that couldn't be seen from the road. I leaned his body up against a huge tree stump and held him there. I could see him very clearly in the moonlight. He had just flickered momentarily into consciousness as I drew the knife across his throat. It was an interesting expression on his face. Bewilderment, not pain, nor shock.

As his life flowed out before me, I was conscious it was not pleasure I felt this time, but relief, the rapid dissipation of unbearable tension.

I went back to the car afterward for a drink and a couple of cigarettes and to figure out just exactly where to bury his body.

This was one body that couldn't be found under any circumstances. Sandusky was where the good Dr. Sweeney went to dry out when the bad Kingsbury Run killer was murdering in Cleveland. I was very careful in disposing of his body, and it took me several hours to do it. Afterward, I went back to the hospital to get some sleep.

What is it, then, that's eating at me? Gnawing a hole in my stomach lining? That I killed this guy? No, that's not it.

It finally hit me. I hadn't fully realized it before, but I can't stop. The need, the lust is in control, and it scares the hell out of me.

I used to think I killed for pleasure. Then I convinced myself I did it for the publicity, but I always thought I could start it and stop it at will. Perhaps at one time, I could. I'll never know.

If I don't stop, one of these days, I'm sure to slip up, and they will catch me. And when they catch me, they will execute me. I don't want to die in the electric chair. I don't want to be a freak everybody is afraid of. I want to live like everyone else with a wife and my children. I want to be a doctor people admire and respect.

I really need to have Jenny with me. She alone can calm my nerves. I can't find her. Wilson said she didn't come into work today, and her landlady says she's not in her room. I hope I can reach her later. If ever I needed her, I need her now.

I don't know where to turn for help now. I don't even know how long I have before this lust will seize me again. Right now, I'd like to drown myself in whiskey and pretend this is all a bad dream.

MARCH 30, 1938

Oh, Jesus Christ! This is the beginning of the end for me. I was listening to the news on the radio this evening, and they found one of his legs in Sandusky. Some goddamn dog dug it up.

Now, what? I've got to get a hold of myself. My whole goddamn life could depend on what happens in the next twenty-four hours.

As soon as the police realize I was out there again in Sandusky, it's all over.

I wish I could get my hands to stop shaking. I've taken as much barbital as I can to calm down. If I take any more, I'll put myself to sleep. I've got too much serious thinking to do tonight to be groggy.

I can't seem to focus my mind properly. One part of me has panicked and wants to get out of the city immediately, maybe even out of the country, before the police put things together. The other part of me says that I'm overreacting to this one bit of news.

There's no point in scaring myself unless they find the rest of his body. Right now, all they have is a leg. For all they know, it could have been removed surgically, or it could be the leg of a man who died from natural causes. There is nothing right now to tie this leg to the Kingsbury Run case or to me.

But the dog is sure to lead them back to the woods where it found the leg in the first place. Then they'll send out a bevy of police to look for places that have been recently dug up. Eventually, they will find the rest of him. That could take another few days. I need to monitor that closely.

If I have to get out of the country, where can I go? I don't have a passport, and I doubt that I have enough time to get one. Canada, maybe. I don't need a passport for Canada. Just a birth certificate, as I remember.

If I had to, I could get the boys and then cross the Canadian border. I could use the money I saved for a house and start over in Canada. It would be easy to get lost in Canada, even with the boys if I practiced outside the bigger cities.

I wonder what it would take to persuade Jenny to go with me. I might be able to convince her that she needs to leave the country to prevent her husband from finding her. I don't know if she'd fall for that or not. Speaking of Jenny, I'd better call her later tonight, when I'm a little more sober. I think she's really pissed at me.

Jesus, of all times for her to drop in here. Right after I heard about this leg in Sandusky. She was so excited about that new job at Higbee's that she's moving into a nicer rooming house. I should be sharing her excitement and celebrating her new job with her. Instead, I'm half in the bag. She was really upset when she saw me. I can understand that. I'll make it up to her tomorrow.

APRIL 1, 1938

I turned on the radio to hear the news and looked through the evening paper. Nothing about Sandusky. When I called Jenny this afternoon, I told her I picked up her suitcase at her old rooming house just like I promised I would and would see her around six-thirty for dinner. Then I'd drive her to her new place and help her get settled.

That was the plan, but she caught me unawares two hours early. This was her last day at Wilson's, and she felt like leaving early. She was upset when she saw the bottle of whiskey on the table and the condition I was in. She turned around and walked to the door. I put down my drink and asked her to please stay. She stopped walking, turned around, and looked angrily at me. She said she didn't understand what was happening to me and that she's afraid I'm just like her ex-husband. I told her I would put away the bottle and not have another drink the whole night if she would just stay with me.

She thought about it for a minute and then she sat down on the couch opposite my desk. She mumbled something I didn't quite hear. Something about Eliot Ness. I asked her to repeat it, but she said it was nothing. I insisted, and she finally did but very reluctantly.

Why is it all the really good men like Eliot Ness are married?

I was confused by her comment. What do you know about Eliot Ness? I asked her. The only time you saw him was at the Hollenden late last year when I pointed him out to you. She had an odd look on her face as though she was deciding what to tell me. I've seen him several times since, she said, watching my face closely.

I picked up my whiskey glass again and drank from it. How is it, I asked her, that you saw him after the dinner at the Hollenden? He didn't speak to you as far as I could tell, and he didn't know your name. She reached over to the desk and took one of my cigarettes. I had never seen her smoke before. She lighted the cigarette, crossed her legs, and sat back on the couch.

It was quite by accident, she said, blowing the smoke at me. I saw him waiting for the elevator in the same building my divorce lawyer is in. He recognized me from the restaurant. She laughed giddily. Can you imagine that? All those months later? Remembering her? She was pleased and flattered by that. Then what happened? I asked her. I could see in her face that she enjoyed talking about him but was embarrassed she had never mentioned it to me. Nothing really happened, she said. He introduced himself to her, as though anybody in this city didn't know who he was.

She said she was very impressed by his humility. Naturally, she returned the courtesy, told him her name, and where she worked. She inhaled again and then blew another cloud of smoke in my direction.

Was that the only time you saw him? I asked her. She looked at me coyly, with just a tiny beginning of a smile on her face. No, she answered. He's dropped by the drugstore several times lately when he was in the neighborhood.

In the neighborhood, I repeated softly, thinking of how out of the way this area is from the places he would normally frequent. I took another drink from my glass and lighted a cigarette for myself.

Have you been out with him yet? I asked as though I were inquiring about whether the mail had been delivered.

She was slow to respond. What do you mean when you say out with?

I laughed and told her I didn't think there were many interpretations to my question. She became very precise when she told me she had lunch with him twice and drinks with him once, but he's never asked her out on a date. He's married, she explained righteously.

I nodded and said nothing. She started to talk again as though she felt it was necessary to explain her relationship. He's Scandinavian, she told me. Norwegian. I've been teaching him little phrases in Danish, which is very similar to Norwegian.

I nodded, drained my glass, and poured another. Would you like one? I offered. She said no. I picked up my drink, walked around from behind my desk, and sat next to her on the couch. I put my drink down on the lamp table and turned toward her, my arm draped over the couch behind her. I gently stroked her long brown hair and looked at her beautiful green eyes. I have done this many times before, and she has always turned her face directly to me and gazed lovingly into my eyes. This time, she didn't. She continued to show me her profile while her eyes darted around nervously, always avoiding mine. My admiration was no longer welcome. It was awkward and superfluous.

Tell me some more about Eliot Ness, I heard myself ask her. What kind of man is he really? She turned and looked surprised at my question. It was a subject she was more than happy to expound on. Her eyes lighted up when she talked about him. You would really like him, she assured me. She went on for several minutes about how kind he was and sensitive, what punishingly long hours he worked and how dangerous his job is.

I said nothing. I didn't listen very closely. My mind was elsewhere. I wanted to ask her how he compared to me in bed, but I don't think I did. But then, she wouldn't have been able to answer me anyway at that time because my hands were already closed around her throat. I'm trying to understand exactly how they got there. I don't remember putting them there. It wasn't my intention to put my hands there, but they were definitely there for such a long time. I tried to take them away, but I couldn't. It was as though my hands were nailed to her throat.

Jesus God. What have I done?

[Note: There are no entries in this volume from April 1, 1938, to May 17, 1938. For that period of time, there were several newspaper clippings about the tenth victim, whose severed leg was found floating in the Cuyahoga River on April 8. May 8, pieces of the victim's torso were found floating in a burlap bag in the Cuyahoga River. She was approximately five feet, two inches tall. Her age was estimated at between twenty-five and thirty years old. Her date of death was estimated to be April 1. Unlike the finesse shown on previous victims, the incisions were cruder and jagged with long, sweeping hesitation marks.]

MAY 17, 1938

Maybe this little drama isn't over yet after all. My old friend Jack from Tony's paid me a visit today. I know he means well, but I wish he would mind his own business. I don't need somebody else to be upset because I drink too much. Maybe I do drink too much. Maybe I am killing myself. Who the hell cares? I mean, who the hell really cares?

Jack didn't come over to the office to lecture me on my drinking, though. He wanted to talk about something with me before he told his boss about it. While I'm not too crazy about him trying to blow the whistle on me, I do appreciate that he warned me first. I understand he has a job to do and can't let minor friendships get in the way.

I always thought Jack was a smart cookie, and now he's proving me right. I really do have to give him credit for using his head. He is the only one in the whole goddamn police force who has figured out any connection between Sandusky and me.

Those other two detectives who came to see me a couple of times never did put it together. Not that I am particularly surprised. I always seem to overestimate the collective intelligence of the police. But old Jack remembered I had been in Sandusky last July when one of the killings took place. Then when he heard about that leg they found out there, he started to draw some conclusions. He said it took him longer than he'd like to admit to figure out what happened and even longer to decide what to do about it.

I asked him what he thought might have happened. He said he'd done some discreet checking around at the veteran's hospital. There were some "alarming coincidences." I couldn't stop from smiling when he said that. He's so damned serious.

He went on talking, visibly disconcerted by my smile. Last July, he said, when the killing occurred in Cleveland, I was theoretically out of town in a hospital. I agreed with that statement, but I told him it was factual, not theoretical.

Yet, Jack said, during the weekend when the killing took place, there was no way to actually prove I was at the hospital. No one specifically remembered me being there the entire weekend. Jack said it was entirely possible for me to have come back to Cleveland in my car that Saturday night, killed the victim, and returned to Sandusky the same night.

I like Jack. I really do. I had to smile again. Finally, I got him to crack a tiny little smile. I poured some whiskey for the two of us and apologized for not having any beer in the icebox.

Then Jack started up again about my last trip to Sandusky at the end of March. He said he spoke with people there at the hospital about me, and they all described me as very agitated. The psychiatrist, bless his dim-witted little soul, said he planned to talk to me in depth when I was rested, but I had checked out before he had the chance.

Jack asked me if I didn't find it a little strange that just after I was out there, a leg was found. And when I got back to Cleveland a few days later, there were parts of a woman's body thrown into the Cuyahoga River.

Interesting story, I told him. I didn't see, however, quite where he was going with it. I told him whether anyone saw me at the hospital that weekend in July was absolutely irrelevant. I was there at the hospital and not in Cleveland. There was no way for him to prove differently.

As for the leg that was found in Sandusky, I was unaware the authorities had even decided it was a homicide. As it stood, that leg could have been the result of legitimate surgery, mutilation of a corpse, or even an accident. The rest of the body had never been found.

I said that the recent decapitated female victim was just one more in the long Kingsbury Run series. I told him I didn't know anything more about that murder than I did about any of the earlier ones. The fact I was in Cleveland when it happened meant nothing. So were thousands of other people, including himself.

Even though I was a bit drunk this afternoon, I think the coolness of my logic made him doubt his suspicions. He said he didn't want to get me in any trouble. He was sure I already had enough of my own to deal with. But, he said he was going to have to say something about these coincidences to his superiors. If I was innocent, he said, then I have nothing at all to worry about. Someone will turn up to substantiate my story.

Jack, I told him firmly, I don't have to have my whereabouts substantiated. First of all, I am a physician, not some bum on the street. Second, the police department does not have one tiny shred of evidence to link me to any crime. Being in the same city is hardly evidence of guilt. While I felt fairly certain of the legalities on that point, I told him I'd double check it with my cousin Martin.

He picked up on what I was saying about Martin. Jack knows what a can of worms he'll open with this revelation of his. Jack said he was sorry for bringing my name into the case. It had troubled him for weeks before he decided to talk to me about it. He added that he liked me a lot and had the deepest admiration for Martin, but he still had to put personal issues aside and do his job. He picked up his jacket off the couch and started to leave.

I stopped him. Jack, I asked him, looking him straight in the eye. What do you think? Do you really believe I could be the Kingsbury Run killer? The Mad Butcher? I put particular emphasis on this ludicrous title the press had given to me.

He met my stare and thought hard about my question. Some days, he said, I think it has to be someone like you. Someone very intelligent and outgoing. Other days, I can't believe someone as sane and normal appearing as you are could possibly have killed all those people. But if you are guilty, I've got to say that you're damned good. Unbelievably good. Frighteningly good at what you do. With that comment, he left.

It was quite a compliment coming from Jack. He's not normally effusive in his praise. In fact, he's quite the opposite. Quick to find the stupidity or incompetence in the people around him. Compliments from Jack are to be treasured.

Any police investigation that might come from Jack's comments will take some time to get off the ground. Let's say Jack talks to Hogan sometime today. Hogan isn't going to do anything unless he gets an okay from Ness. Boy, could that create some fireworks. Martin would be down on Eliot Ness in minutes. Martin would see any investigation of me as being political vengeance for him making the Kingsbury Run case such a potent campaign issue in the last election. And Martin would see it as an attempt to discredit him as a candidate for mayor in the next election.

It goes beyond politics, though. Hogan doesn't want to believe a good Irish lad like myself, who bootstrapped himself into being a doctor, is some crazy killer. Nor does he want to believe the first cousin of his own "working man's hero," Martin Sweeney, is guilty of such crimes. Hogan knows how hard it was for our people to fight for respectability in this city. If I were Hogan, I'd try to ignore this young detective and his scandalous insinuations about a member of a good, solid Irish family.

It'll take at least a week for all of that shit to percolate in their coffee pots. Afterward, Hogan may decide to do nothing at all. On the other hand, a very perfunctory investigation may be done to put the entire matter to bed officially. But then, if that Eliot Ness gets involved, there could be one hell of a detailed investigation. I'd better be prepared for the worst.

MAY 26, 1938
More than a week has gone by, and I haven't seen any tangible results from Jack's threat. No one has been here to see me, and I'm fairly certain I'm not being followed.

Just in case this investigation does materialize, I've had time to think up some very clever ways to entertain myself. I haven't heard a peep from Martin yet so that button hasn't been pushed. Maybe this whole thing has died in committee.

JUNE 3, 1938

Just when I had given up on the police, four of them appeared on my doorstep this morning. For a couple of weeks now, ever since Jack's visit, I've made a wildly successful effort to stay reasonably sober all day. That is, until five o'clock. It simply would not do for me to be drunk when the police question me on capital offenses.

There were the two detectives who were here twice before, the illustrious David Cowles, Ness's forensic expert and trusted lieutenant, and some other guy in his early fifties who was dressed better than most cops.

I brought in a chair from my waiting room, and we all crowded into my study. Three of them sat on my couch and Cowles sat on the chair. I sat behind my desk and quickly put the whiskey bottle and glass that had been sitting on the desk in the drawer. It looked so unbelievably gauche for a liquor bottle to be sitting there nakedly on my desk so early in the morning.

Cowles did almost all the talking, except for a couple of questions from the guy in the expensive suit. They questioned me for about an hour and a half, covering a wide range of things. Questions on my personal and professional life as well as where was I on a certain day, months, and even years ago.

I fought down that need of mine to grandstand, to play to an audience. I didn't crack any jokes, even though there were a couple straining so hard to get loose I was almost foaming at the mouth. Instead, I was very restrained, reflective, cooperative, and serious. Just a touch of nervousness initially.

When they were finished with their questions, Cowles asked if they could have a brief look around the office, and I became much more visibly nervous. I asked Cowles if he had a search warrant. He was prepared for the question. He said he didn't ask to search the office, merely to take a look around.

My hands started to shake. He noticed. I hesitated and said I wasn't sure if what he was asking was legal. He said if I was concerned about the legality, he would have someone over here in five minutes with a search warrant. What a splendid bluff. Five minutes. He must think I'm extremely naive. Very reluctantly, with anxiety clearly in my voice, I agreed to let him take a look around.

There were only two other rooms to see, the examining room, and the surgery. First, I showed them the examining room, which is very small. There is nothing much to see in there.

Then we all walked into the surgery. This was the room that held their interest. One of the detectives rushed to the icebox and opened it. He seemed very disappointed when all he found was the remnants of the sandwich I bought for last night's dinner.

The operating table was in the center of the room. I explained that it was here that I did very minor operations, like removing hemorrhoids. I betrayed my anxiousness to get them out of there, but they stayed.

At one end of the room was a screen with another table on wheels behind it. One of the detectives looked behind the screen and motioned to the rest of them to come over. Cowles moved the screen aside so they could all see what was on the table. It looked like a bulky male body was lying there on the table, covered with a bloody sheet.

They froze for a minute, all standing around the table with their eyes fixed on the sheet. None of them touched it. After what seemed like an eternity, Cowles yanked the sheet off the table. For another minute, all they did was gape at what was lying under the sheet.

Finally, Cowles touched it. It's papier-mâché, he said, grasping the arm of the headless, dismembered, human-like form I had molded together. Cowles turned and glared at me. He was not amused.

All that nervousness I had shown before melted into an innocent smile. Do you like it? I asked. It's a hobby of mine, molding these forms out of papier-mâché. Helps me keep my anatomical skills in top shape.

Cowles didn't fall for that explanation. Not that I expected him to. My little trick infuriated him. Did your cousin put you up to this or was it your own idea? He wanted to know. I pretended not to know what he was talking about.

The only one of the four who had any appreciation for the humor in my little paper and plaster creation was the guy in the nice suit. I saw the smile cross his face while he listened to my brief, unpleasant exchange with Cowles. He watched my face intently until they all left, but he never said a word to me or to the others. I wonder now just who he was. He didn't seem much like a cop to me. Maybe he was one of Burton's stooges from city hall. After all, this whole investigation carries a significant political risk for Burton and Ness both.

JUNE 13, 1938

I think there's a police investigation of me going on, but it's being done very discreetly. I saw Driscoll yesterday at Dugan's, and he said there was a guy in the bar a few days ago asking about me. Driscoll said he never identified himself or gave a reason for asking all the questions.

I was curious about what they were asking. A lot of general things, Driscoll said. Did I have a girlfriend? How much did I drink? What caused Mary to leave me? Driscoll said he didn't really know me that well and couldn't answer any personal questions, so the guy left.

Maybe I was right about them just doing a perfunctory investigation. There's not really much more for them to do except cover all the same old ground again they covered some months ago. I may not be leading the life of a Bible hero, but it doesn't mean I'm a killer either.

JUNE 29, 1938

Last month I explained to Hurley that I had some problems to address before I take on a larger workload. I didn't want the cops to come sniffing around his office. Hurley's a decent guy, and he doesn't need to hear that I'm a murder suspect.

I only have the few patients who come into this office. Time is heavy on my hands. I'm sorry in a way my little adventure with the police department has died down. It provided some real diversion for me. But, they seem to have lost interest.

Just to let them know I'm still alive, I sent off a postcard to Lieutenant Cowles. It had a photo of the skyline of downtown Cleveland, the kind that a tourist would buy. On the back of the postcard, I carefully drew a picture of the morgue. And just above the door on the morgue, I drew the sign "No More Bodies" and signed the card Frank Sweeney. Jenny's body was the last. I wonder if that old sourpuss Cowles will get the humor in it right away. He must have seen that "No More Bodies" sign they put on the morgue door when there were no more cadavers available for the medical school.

JULY 6, 1938

I finally got a response to my postcard to Mr. Cowles. He's put a tail on me. I noticed it when I went downtown to Higbee's to buy some socks. I became aware of this guy who was watching me. At first, I thought it was the store detective who had taken me for a shoplifter.

Then, when I went over to the May Company, I saw the same guy watching me again. I didn't do anything right away. I let him follow me around for a while. Then, when I was leaving the men's department, I ducked behind the corner wall by the elevator and waited for him to walk by.

When he walked by, I followed him. He didn't notice immediately. But when he realized I wasn't in front of him anymore, he quickly looked around. That's when he saw me behind him, grinning from ear to ear.

He's a young fellow. No more than twenty-five. As Irish as Paddy's pig. I went up to him and asked him his name. Tommy Whelan, he stuttered. Pleased to meet you, Tommy, I said. As you know, I'm Frank Sweeney. If we're going to be hanging around much together, we might as well be introduced.

His face fell a mile, humiliated by his failure. He had obviously been too clumsy in following me. I hadn't thought about that when I played that little game on him. Then I felt sorry for him. He seemed like such a nice lad. Don't worry, I told him. I won't let on to anybody you're following me. He was relieved, but I could tell he felt a bit foolish. He shook my hand and waved me ahead of him. Afterward, he followed me at a respectable distance.

JULY 30, 1938

Tommy Whelan is still following me during the day, but there are replacements for him on the weekends and at night. I feel quite safe these days with all this police protection. I wonder how long they'll keep this up. It must be getting quite expensive.

I think tonight I'm going to take advantage of this unsolicited accompaniment and visit a couple of those colored dives on Quincy Avenue I never had the guts to go into alone. Won't that be something now? Two little snow-white faces in an all-colored bar. Just me and my shadow, except my shadow isn't going to be dark. I hope we both don't get killed.

P.S. We didn't get killed, but we sure got some strange looks. He sat down at the other end of the bar. As I expected, we were the only two whites in the whole place. I saw how very uncomfortable he was, so I sent a drink down to him and toasted his health. This cop doesn't have the sense of humor that Tommy has.

AUGUST 17, 1938

They finally found the little gift I left under Eliot Ness's office window. Too bad the cretins in the coroner's office didn't realize her body had been embalmed, not frozen. I wonder whose bones were nearby. Not anybody that I knew.

[Note: Slipped in between the pages of the journal were two newspaper articles. One was the entire front page which was dominated by the discovery of two dismembered bodies found at a downtown dump. One of the corpses was a woman, who had been dead for about six months, but whose body was in good condition because it had been refrigerated. The other was the skeleton of a man who had been dead nine months. Police estimated the bodies had been at the dump for three weeks. The other article had a very unfavorable story about the raid Eliot Ness initiated on Shantytown on August 16th when he tried to rid the city of the source of the murder victims by burning down all the shacks and jailing the hobos. Dr.

Frank Sweeney had an office at 5040 Broadway next to a funeral home that had a contract to bury indigent and unclaimed bodies. In a 1983 interview, Lieutenant David Cowles said he had testimony that the doctor would go over to the place where the indigent bodies were kept and perform amputations.]

AUGUST 24, 1938

I was out cold on my couch that fateful morning five days ago, still very drunk from my tour of the saloons that ended around two a.m., when I heard loud knocking on the door to my waiting room. I looked at my watch. It wasn't even eight o'clock in the morning yet. I wondered who the hell would make that kind of racket so early in the morning.

I rolled off the couch, knocked my glasses on the floor in the process, and yelled at the top of my lungs for whoever it was to keep their goddamn pants on while I looked for mine. Once I picked up my glasses, I saw my trousers lying on the floor exactly where I dropped them several hours ago. I went to put them on but almost fell over trying. Fuck it all to hell, I said, staggering to the door in my underwear.

It was Lieutenant Cowles and Tommy Whelan. Cowles was very serious and formal in spite of the informality of my dress. We need to take you in for questioning, he said. It would be best if you got dressed now. I don't know if I even answered them. I just staggered to the toilet and let go. I wasn't feeling well at all that morning.

My memory of what happened right afterward is very spotty. I must have somehow gotten dressed. Either that or the two of them put my clothes on me. I hope it didn't happen that way. I would hate to think I was so drunk I had to have the cops dress me.

I must have passed out again in their car because I don't remember riding with them downtown. Nor do I have any recollection of going with them into the lobby of the Cleveland Hotel.

The next thing I remember was sitting on the leather couch in a very fancy oak-paneled living room that was part of a hotel suite. Sitting in a chair, pulled up right opposite me, was the nice-looking, middle-aged man in the expensive suit who had come to my office with Cowles and the two detectives back in June. I remember at the time that he didn't seem like a cop. Actually, he wasn't a cop. He introduced himself to me as Dr. Royal Grossman, the court psychiatrist.

Not far from me in this sumptuous drawing room sat Lieutenant Cowles. Tommy Whelan was standing by the door. Cowles politely asked him if he would be kind enough to wait outside in the hall. Stay near the door, Whelan, Cowles instructed him softly, in case you're needed.

I can't believe I didn't notice him right away, considering how vividly he stands out in both my memory and imagination. But there he was, standing across the room, looking out the window. Eliot Ness in the flesh. Even in my sorry, inebriated state, I was lucid enough to be excited that finally, the Great Man had taken a personal interest in me. I despised myself for that fleeting feeling, but I felt it none the less.

In retrospect, had I been more sober, I would have realized the day I came face to face with Eliot Ness about the Kingsbury Run murders was the day my future was in grave peril. Like the deeply religious man who yearns to be closer to God and is thrilled one day to wake up facing his maker, only to realize now he is dead. Not that Ness and I have quite that type of hierarchical relationship, but the outcome is analogous.

We're going to have to dry him out first, Eliot, I heard Dr. Grossman say to him. Ness turned from the window and looked at the psychiatrist and at me. How long will that take? Ness was impatient. Dr. Grossman told him probably three full days, maybe a little longer.

Damn it! Ness said. I hadn't planned on that. I suppose we have to find some way of keeping him here through Sunday night, but it could get real sticky for me.

I'll give him a sedative, Dr. Grossman told him. It will keep him relatively calm until he gets the alcohol out of his system. I don't want him getting the shakes too bad. Have a couple of your men keep an eye on him. I'll leave a telephone number where you can reach me. I'll be back here again, he said, later today to give him some more medication.

Shortly after, I felt Dr. Grossman giving me an injection. I wanted to protest, to call my cousin, but I knew it was too late. I started to feel drowsy almost immediately. I remember thinking, just before I fell asleep, how glad I was they wouldn't start questioning me until I was completely sober. That was a big relief to me, and I nodded off relatively happy.

Somehow they got me undressed and into an enormous bed in one of the two bedrooms of the hotel suite. I completely lost track of time. They kept me sedated until Sunday evening. Even with the sedatives, my nerves were absolutely raw. Nobody, who has not gone through it, can possibly understand what kind of mental and physical torture it is to be suddenly deprived of any liquor when it has been the mainstay of your existence for years. The body rebels. It fights back. The mind looks to find any way to steal or beg a drink.

Those three days were absolute hell. Yes, I'd been through it once before when I first went out to Sandusky, but being through it once doesn't in any way make it easier the second time. At least they didn't take me off the barbital at the same time.

I couldn't stay put for five minutes at a time. I tried to relax in one of those luxurious chairs and look out the window, but I couldn't sit still. Then I tried to lie down in that big comfortable bed, but I couldn't sleep. I took warm showers and hot baths to try to quiet my nerves, but it didn't work. I ended up pacing around the suite for hours on end.

Addiction is so degrading. I would have done absolutely anything for Whelan if he would have gotten some whiskey for me. I pleaded with him, played on his sympathy, offered him money, just for one shot. He wouldn't do it, though.

Thank God, the craving started to subside considerably by Sunday evening. The sedative had worn off, and I was becoming alert again. I joked with Whelan about the fancy hotel suite. I told him the department must be handing out a lot of speeding tickets to afford this place for a couple of nights. He laughed and said Ness was probably getting the suite at no charge. He had a lot of friends around town in high places.

Whelan asked me what I'd like to eat. He was having dinner brought up for the other cop and himself. It made sense for them to order my dinner at the same time. It wasn't often I get to eat a free Sunday dinner in a fancy hotel like that, so I ordered the works. Shrimp cocktail. Onion soup. Sirloin steak and mashed potatoes. Cherry pie for dessert. And, I reminded Whelan when I gave him the order, not to forget the bottle of French champagne. He laughed. While I waited for dinner, I took a shower and put on some of the clean clothes they had brought from my office.

Everything came as ordered except, of course, for the champagne. Someone had substituted a pot of coffee instead. Whelan said I'd want to have my wits about me that night. Why? I asked him. What did he have planned for the evening's entertainment? He rolled his eyes up toward the ceiling and said that Ness, Cowles, and Dr. Grossman would be there around eight o'clock to ask me the questions I wasn't "well enough," as he put it delicately, to answer a few days before. That certainly gave me something to look forward to.

It wasn't long before the dinners were delivered. The food was excellent, and I was ravenously hungry. I hadn't eaten any serious solid food since Thursday afternoon. I had the plate licked clean within twenty minutes or so, which gave me an hour and a half to enjoy my coffee, digest my food, and smoke a couple of cigarettes before my inquisitors descended upon me.

I thought about calling Martin and telling him the bad news. I knew that in the next day or so I would have to talk to him. It was a call I didn't relish making, so I decided I wouldn't ruin his and Marie's Sunday night unless something happened that made his presence absolutely necessary.

I still felt a bit groggy from the sedatives, but they were wearing off quickly enough. The coffee did a lot to revive me. All in all, I was in pretty good shape to stand up to the team coming to work on me. I would have absolutely killed for a drink, though. Yes, killed for one.

I wasn't as nervous as I would have expected myself to be. I was deliberately being treated with kid gloves. No hot, glaring lights in a windowless room in the police station. No confession was beaten out of me with a rubber truncheon. No, this was all very, very civilized, at least for the time being. I was, after all, a physician, not some hobo in shantytown. And, most importantly, I was Martin's cousin. Ness quite rightly must have assumed that every detail of my capture would be relayed to Martin. Any hint of illegality or mistreatment would hit the front page of the paper.

Ness was the first of them to arrive. It was a few minutes before eight. He was dressed in a suit and tie, looking like he'd just come from dinner at some fancy restaurant. The first thing he did was take off his suit coat and tie, which he tossed over the back of the chair, and rolled up his shirt sleeves.

When he saw me sitting on the couch in the living room, drinking my coffee, he came over and introduced himself. He was very friendly, almost casual. He took out a package of cigarettes from his shirt pocket and offered me one. I took it.

He said I looked a whole lot better than I did when he first saw me and asked how I was feeling. I told him I was feeling a lot better than I was a few days earlier. I didn't want to tell him my whole body was screaming for a drink. Instead, I lighted the cigarette and enjoyed the meager comfort of the only addiction I could indulge.

Ness thanked me for being so cooperative those past three days. He said he appreciated how difficult they were for me physically and emotionally. I seriously doubted a man like himself had any grasp of just how hard it had been for me.

He went on to say there were some very important questions he needed to ask me, and it was critical that I was completely sober when I answered them. He said he hoped I was comfortable there in the hotel, in spite of the inconvenience.

I was surprised by how sincere and friendly he seemed to be. I was beginning to wonder if I had misjudged him. In spite of his friendliness, I knew that I'd better not let down my guard or I would find myself in jail for life or worse. I crushed the cigarette butt in the ashtray and immediately lighted another one from the pack Ness had left on the coffee table. I hated myself for doing it. I don't like to broadcast my dependencies, especially to the enemy camp, but the cigarettes were a way of transporting my nervousness from my head down to my fingertips and out into the cigarette, or so it seemed.

Ness said he was going to order some more coffee before the others arrived. I listened as he called down to room service. His voice was a perfect reflection of his person. Confident, commanding, but friendly and patient. Unusual in a person so young.

It's very difficult for me to be around that man. He made me unbearably tense. I couldn't forget Jenny preferred him to me. And with some good reason, it pains me to finally admit it. It's a wound that just won't close.

While my intense jealousy is certainly at the core of this deep conflict with Ness, it's not the only factor. Even before Jenny, I had those secret ups and downs in my crazy, one-sided relationship with him. It was all in my head. None of it was real.

Fed by my frustrations over the way he treated the murders with such disdain and fanned by Martin's vocal dislike of him, it was so easy to hate him without knowing him at all. It was much more difficult to dislike him in person. He is just too compelling a personality. I feel pretty stupid about the whole thing.

Cowles arrived shortly thereafter. He was also dressed in a suit and tie. Cowles's only concession to the heat was to take off his suit coat and park himself in the chair directly opposite the larger fan. Cowles kept on his tie. No rolled-up shirtsleeves on him. He was dressed for work that Sunday night. The last one to come was Dr. Grossman. He was perspiring heavily and kept mopping his face with his handkerchief.

Ness started the conversation. Dr. Sweeney, he said, as you know, the series of murders known as the Kingsbury Run killings has plagued this city for several years now. It is my highest priority to solve these crimes and bring this killing spree, as he called it, to an end.

He looked me straight in the eye and spoke frankly. He said they had a number of questions they'd like to ask me that night and possibly the next morning. He hoped I would answer them satisfactorily.

On the other hand, I interjected with a smile, if I don't answer the questions satisfactorily, you'll throw me in jail. Is that it? Ness answered quickly. He didn't want the session to start out antagonistically, particularly when I had been so cooperative up until then. He knew at any time, I could insist on calling my lawyer and refuse to answer any questions without him. Ness was very firm, but cordial when he said that, as keen as he was to solve the murders, he never had people jailed without very substantial reasons. I was half tempted to mention the poor tramps he picked up in his shantytown raid and threw in jail on the flimsiest of charges, but then I wasn't particularly interested in being antagonistic either.

Dr. Grossman took over at that point. He was very conciliatory and used his smooth voice to put me at ease. We'd like to ask you some very detailed questions about your personal and professional life. I recognize you have already gone over some of this information with various people in the department, but please bear with us on the questions that seem repetitive.

He was right. Most of the questions they asked me over the next few hours I had already answered before, at least, to some extent. On the other hand, what was very different this time was Dr. Grossman's probing and emphasis on the things that interested him. It was also very clear to me they had been asking quite a number of people some very personal questions about me.

Like the questions on my marriage. I had told them it had broken up because my wife and I had different values, plus she didn't like me drinking after work with my friends. Dr. Grossman approached the subject from an entirely different perspective, one that he could have only gotten from Mary herself. It was our sexual relationship he wanted to talk about.

It pissed me off that he had talked to her. It also angered me he would bring up something so personal and from my viewpoint, so irrelevant, in front of Ness and Cowles. I didn't show my anger. Instead, I smiled.

I think he took it for granted Mary was telling him the truth when she said we hadn't slept together for some months before we separated. Did I have a girlfriend then? he asked. Did I use prostitutes during my marriage? Was impotence a problem?

I told Dr. Grossman that before he jumped to any conclusions about my sex life with my ex-wife, he needed to have a much better understanding of both Mary's physical charms and her personality. Being a gentleman, I said, I would never say disparaging things about the mother of my children. However, there were aspects of my ex-wife which could not be fully conveyed in a simple telephone conversation. Dr. Grossman cracked a smile, took a couple of notes, and went on to the next subject.

He shifted the focus to my father. They had really done some digging on that subject. Some of the things even I didn't know or didn't remember. Of course, they had access to the police and social welfare files. I gather my father was pretty well documented. And, of course, there were years of psychiatric files from when they locked him up at Cleveland State Hospital.

I agreed my father was a violent psychotic, but I hoped Dr. Grossman was not suggesting my father's psychosis was directly heritable like blue eyes and brown hair. Directly heritable? No, Dr. Grossman didn't believe that any more than I did. However, he said there was very strong empirical evidence that alcoholism and the violence which so often accompanies it ran in families.

The next hour was spent rehashing my experiences during the war and my professional life after the incident with Mullens.

Again, it was obvious to me they had been very thorough in their investigation during the past few months. They must have talked to a lot of people and looked at a great many documents. I was surprised they had gone to so much trouble.

Dr. Grossman was very interested in the sudden resurgence of my career that started in the fall of last year and came to a halt this past April. Why, he wanted to know, did this frenzy of work begin and end so abruptly and unexpectedly. Did it have anything to do with the pretty young girl I was dating?

I looked over at Ness. He was slouched in his armchair, only half listening at that point. Cowles, however, was listening to every word. What was her name again? Dr. Grossman asked. Cowles supplied the answer before I had a chance to speak. Jenny Petersen, he said.

I watched Ness's reaction. His eyes opened wide, and he sat up straight in his chair. What'd you say her name was? he asked Cowles. Cowles repeated it. Ness stared at me. I could tell it dawned on him where he'd seen me before. He finally recognized me as the man who was Jenny's escort last December at the Hollenden. Our eyes met. He frowned and switched the toothpick to the other side of his mouth, thinking over the ramifications of what he had just learned.

Dr. Grossman spoke. Yes, he said, this Petersen girl. Tell me about her. Where did you meet here? When did you start going out with her? Is the relationship still going on?

I downplayed the subject very calmly. I directed my comments to Ness, occasionally acknowledging the other two. I said that we dated for several months, but, and I looked Ness straight in the eyes, she had other boyfriends. Ness looked extremely uncomfortable. I told them I was very wrapped up in my work at that time, and I didn't have much time for her. I said the reason for my sudden interest in work was that I believed I would be able to have my boys live with me, so I needed to increase my income to provide a good home for them. I said that all of a sudden I didn't know how to get in touch with Jenny anymore. She had found a new job somewhere and had moved out of her rooming house. I told them I was too busy then to spend any time trying to track her down.

Cowles quizzed me on what I knew about her background and where she was from. I said I knew very little about her and had the feeling she was covering up something about her past. I looked over at Ness and told him if she had meant more to me, I would have taken the trouble to find out more about her.

Dr. Grossman asked me again why I suddenly stopped working so hard a few months ago if it wasn't related to this girl leaving me. I said when it became clear to me that I couldn't have my boys come live with me after all, my motivation to make a lot of money had vanished.

Looking back on that evening, I realize now the first two hours were questions that helped Dr. Grossman complete his psychological profile of me. He asked all the questions and took most of the notes on what I said. The rest of the evening, which went on for almost three more hours, was a series of questions, put to me mostly by Cowles, about what I was doing and where I was on certain days and nights around the time of the murders. They had snatched my office appointment books from 1935 through this year to help refresh my memory. Good thing I kept my journals under the floor boards in the closet or they might have snatched them too.

I seriously doubt anything I said was very useful to them in establishing my guilt or innocence. For the most part, I answered that I didn't remember what I was doing on any particular day or night, months and years ago. Finally, they finished with me. I couldn't imagine anything had been left unasked. I told Ness I assumed I could go back to my office the next morning. No, he said. He would need to question me in the morning, as well.

I told him I wasn't going to answer any more questions until I had talked to a lawyer. Since I didn't have a lawyer, I would call Martin in the morning. Ness winced slightly but must have been expecting Martin's involvement sooner or later.

The three of them left me with my police guard and said they would be back around nine the next morning. The cop on duty was a new guy. I hadn't met him before. Whelan must have been sent home for the rest of the night. My mind seized on the opportunity of getting something, even Sunday beer, to drink.

They must not have briefed this new guy at all because he was perfectly willing to let me telephone down to room service for something to drink. I was so excited I could hardly dial the phone. It rang and rang and rang. Then I looked at my watch and saw that it was one o'clock in the morning. Everything had been closed for hours.

I didn't warm to that news. I paced around for another hour, chain smoking, drinking tepid coffee, and trying to figure out how I could get a drink. Finally, I gave it up and climbed into bed. I would need to get some sleep if they were going to fire more questions at me the next day.

The next morning at eight o'clock, I was on the phone with Martin at his home. When I told him where I was and why, I thought he was going to have a stroke right on the spot. First, he swore at Ness, then at the mayor, and then at me for not calling him days ago when the police first picked me up. When he finally calmed down, I told him they were going to start questioning me again in an hour. He made me swear I would not utter a syllable until he got there.

About eight-fifteen, I heard the guard letting in Cowles, Dr. Grossman, and two other men. They went right into the other bedroom in the suite, the one that had been locked since I had been there.

I shut the door to my bedroom so that I could call Agnes and talk to her in private. I called her because I was concerned that she didn't know where I was. It's rare that I don't get in touch with her every few days or so. I told her jokingly where I was. I said all the doctors in the city were being investigated as possible suspects in the series of murders.

Her reaction was not what I expected. She said very little and seemed quite calm, almost resigned. She told me she was going to call Martin before he left home. I gathered at the time she wanted to be sure he would take care of me from a legal standpoint. I told her not to worry, I expected all the excitement would be over shortly, and I'd be by to see her that afternoon.

When I finished talking to Agnes, I could hear them all talking behind the closed door of the other bedroom which was across the hall from mine. My curiosity was getting the better of me. Being a nosy sonofabitch, I pushed the door open and walked in.

When I looked into the room, I almost jumped out of my skin. There were four men in the bedroom. All of them standing around a strange-looking chair with a lot of wires and other apparatus connected to it. The most ghastly notion ran through my mind. This chair and its wires and cables was an electric chair. They had decided I was guilty, and they were going to execute me right there, secretly, without any trial.

What the hell is that? I asked.

Cowles answered that it was a polygraph machine, a lie detector. Then he introduced the two men in the lab coats as Mr. Keeler and his assistant, both from Chicago. I shook hands with them, a little apprehensively.

It was a crazy idea, the electric chair. But this polygraph machine was almost as unnerving. I had read about it. As I recalled, there were serious doubts about its accuracy. For that reason, it wasn't used much.

I asked Dr. Grossman if he was thinking of using that contraption on me?

Dr. Grossman looked a little embarrassed. Oh, you'll find it fascinating, he said, recovering his smoothness. He had Keeler explain to me how the machine worked. It sounded like bullshit to me. I had no confidence some machine would be able to tell if I was lying.

A few minutes later, in walked Eliot Ness, looking dapper and refreshed. He inquired politely if I had slept well and if I'd had a good breakfast. I told him I had. Shall we begin then? he asked. I see you have already inspected our little toy from Chicago, he said with a broad grin.

I smiled back at him. Eliot, I said pleasantly, we're not quite ready to begin anything yet. My cousin Martin had expressed a strong interest in being part of our dialogue, and I promised we'd all wait for him.

Ness was ready for that one. Excellent, he said. I'll order some more coffee and rolls. Martin drinks tea and not coffee, as I recall. I was impressed that Ness would remember such small, personal details about a man he didn't even like.

Martin got there about twenty minutes later. I had prepared myself for quite a display of oratorical histrionics, for which Martin is so well known, but he surprised me. He was very calm and controlled, almost like the senior partner in a very fancy law firm. He told Ness he wanted to talk with him privately. Ness suggested the living room.

I watched Martin's expression as he looked at the expensive surroundings. This was the enemy's territory, the luxurious atmosphere to which Eliot Ness had become accustomed. It was an unfamiliar battleground for Martin. His territory was the church hall, the veterans lodge, the loading dock, the tavern. Still, this was not a battle Martin initiated. The field was not one for him to choose. This was a surprise attack, aimed at his family and reputation.

Martin sat in the armchair opposite the couch where I sat. Ness poured some tea for him and some coffee for himself and me. Martin started the conversation very cordially. What is it, Eliot, he asked him gently, that brings all of us here today?

Martin, Ness responded carefully, I'm sorry to have to be the one to tell you this, but we have reason to believe your cousin could be the man responsible for the Kingsbury Run murders. Martin's face turned bright red, but his voice didn't reflect any of the anger I knew was boiling up in him. Reason? Martin repeated. Would you be kind enough, Eliot, to share with me your reason for believing something so preposterous?

This would be the first time I heard all the evidence they had collected against me. I was pretty nervous about whatever I was going to hear next.

Ness lighted a cigarette and began. Let's start, he said, with the obvious fit between Frank and the profile we have constructed of the killer. Medical training. Large and powerful build. Addiction to alcohol and drugs, which in Frank's case is barbiturates. Lonely lifestyle. An office in the Kingsbury Run area which has the facilities to dismember a body. An automobile to transport the body to various parts of the city. At least occasional fits of temper. Frequent dealings with the lowest levels of society from which the victims were chosen.

Ness paused for a minute to let Martin reflect on what he had just said. Martin did so without any emotion registering on his face. Go on, please, Eliot, he said. There must be more.

Ness took a photograph out of his coat pocket and handed it to Martin. Martin looked at it and gave it to me. It was a picture of me standing with Driscoll, taken, as I recall, at the hospital anniversary dinner six or seven years ago. It was quite a good likeness of me. I handed back the photograph to Ness.

Ness continued to hold the photo in his hand as he spoke. We showed this picture, he said, along with the pictures of several other men, to people who were with the victims just before they disappeared. One of the people was at the bar where Flo Polillo was last seen in January of 1936. He saw and talked to the man Flo was sitting with the last time she was seen alive. The man, Ness said to my cousin, picked Frank as the one he saw in the bar that night.

A man who said he remembered from two and a half years ago? January of 1936? Martin asked incredulously. Quite a good memory, I should think. You mentioned several people. Who were the others?

Ness said the other people were a friend of Edward Andrassy and a bartender who were in the bar where he was last seen alive. Both of them recalled a man who looked like Frank talking to Andrassy in the bar that night.

Martin thought about it for a minute and asked a few questions. Eliot, he said smoothly, you say these two men looked at Frank's picture also. Did each separately pick Frank out among pictures of a number of men? Ness looked a little embarrassed. He said they had a new detective working on it that night who didn't realize he was supposed to show pictures of more than just Frank.

Martin suppressed a smile, but I could see it teasing the corners of his mouth. Let me understand this a little better, Martin said evenly. Your detective took this picture to each man and asked if he had seen Frank that night? Ness mumbled something I could barely hear. Martin was closer to him though and rephrased what he thought he heard. Are you telling me, Eliot, that this ace detective of yours called both men down to the station, sat them in a room together, and showed them the picture of Frank? Ness nodded sheepishly.

Martin was on a roll. Next, Eliot, you're going to tell me both these men also remember back to January of 1936. Actually, it was September of 1935, Ness said quietly. Martin looked over at me and winked.

For a while there, it seemed as though Martin was almost enjoying himself, but the rest of the conversation wasn't nearly as sanguine. Ness informed Martin of the circumstances and coincidences of my trips to the veterans hospital in Sandusky, including the mysterious leg that was discovered there. Martin listened closely and frowned slightly. I was desperate for a drink. It took all the strength I could muster to hide my uneasiness.

The most uncomfortable part of the conversation came last. Ness told Martin the department was still trying to locate my ex-girlfriend, Jenny Petersen, who vanished at the beginning of April. They were also investigating whether she may have been the female victim found in April. Martin looked at me quizzically. His frown deepened.

I felt I needed to throw a little cold water on all their circumstantial evidence and to demonstrate some degree of innocence. I directed my comment to Ness. Eliot, I said, if you think I may be the Kingsbury Run killer, how do you explain those last two bodies you found at the dump a few days ago? The coroner said they'd only been there a couple of weeks. You know, as well as I do, your men have been tailing me night and day since June. And, during that period, your men, including Cowles and Dr. Grossman, have looked through my office fairly closely. Where would I have been able to store the bodies of two people who had been dead so many months? And when would I have had the opportunity to put those remains in the dump without your men seeing me? I watched Martin's face. It was a mixture of surprise and relief. He was probably shocked I never told him the police had come to my office several times or that they were following me.

Newspaper stories to the contrary, Ness said, there are some doubts now as to whether those last two bodies were part of the Kingsbury Run series. In fact, he added, the department was investigating the owner of an embalming college to see if he or any of his students may have been perpetrating some kind of prank.

How convenient for you, said Martin. My cousin has an airtight alibi for two of the killings, and suddenly you decide they're not part of the series. Come now, Eliot, you'll have to do better than that.

Martin, Ness interjected, wanting to get control over the conversation, you asked me why we were all here this morning. We're here to question Frank. This morning, I have arranged for Frank to take a polygraph test. I had an old associate of mine, Mr. Keeler, come all the way from Chicago to test Frank. His equipment and his expertise are unmatched in this country.

Ness looked at his watch. I could tell he was tired of sparring with Martin. He was impatient. Martin, he said, we can clear up a lot of this ambiguity with the polygraph. Let's get it over with.

Martin wasn't one to be hustled by anyone, particularly Eliot Ness. He told Ness he didn't think it was necessary for his cousin to take the test at all. Martin didn't see any particular advantage in having me go through all that just to help the police department screen its suspects.

The kid gloves came off very quickly. Every hint of cordiality disappeared from Ness's voice. He told Martin he'd gone to a great deal of trouble and departmental expense to conduct their interrogation in complete privacy. He said he extended this courtesy because he was sensitive to the reputation of Martin, me, and our family. If I cooperated and was vindicated by the polygraph test, there would never be any record I was ever questioned about the murders.

On the other hand, if I refused to take the polygraph test, I would be taken down to Central Police Station and treated like any other murder suspect. An unpleasant smile appeared on his face. Ness said he couldn't promise the newspapers wouldn't make it into a major story. I could see the pain on Martin's face when he thought about what a carnival the press would turn that news into. I'll have a few words alone with my cousin, he told Ness. The two of us went into my bedroom.

How do you feel about this polygraph? he asked me. I shrugged and said I wasn't sure. Don't worry about it, he assured me, there's no way they can use it in court as evidence.

So you think I should take it? I asked Martin.

Frank, he said solemnly, if you don't take it, all of us lose in a big way. Think about it for a minute. You know Ness will have the reporters crawling up his ass for the details. Your picture will be on the front page. Everybody will think you're the killer, no matter what happens if it ever goes to trial. Think of how Agnes and Sis will feel. And how your boys will feel when they hear of it. My career will be hurt badly, too, he said, but don't think about me. I'll survive.

The worst of it is that you will be a pawn in a political battle between City Hall and myself. They are trying to get at me through you, he said. But it's your career as a doctor that will be shot. Nobody will go to a doctor who's been accused of a horrible string of murders.

My advice to you, Frank, is to take the goddamn test and get them off your back. There's not much they can do to you then. It'll prove they're on the wrong track, and it'll save all of us from a lot of misery.

You're sure they can't use the test in court? I asked him again. He said there was no doubt in his mind. What if the machine's all screwed up or they tamper with it, and it looks like I'm guilty? I asked. It wouldn't make any difference, Martin said, they still can't use it as evidence.

I thought about it for a few minutes. If I refused the test, I would be treated like a criminal. That didn't bother me so much, but dragging poor Agnes and Martin and the rest of the family through that kind of ordeal was more than I could bear. There was always the possibility I would be able to completely fool the machine. I felt confident there wasn't any goddamn machine smarter than I was.

I tried to think through what might happen if they found out from the test I was guilty. The worst that could happen, since they couldn't use the test in court, was that they would search until they were able to come up with some bit of evidence which would stand up in court. Jenny was my weakest link on that score. But then, Eliot Ness was likely to do that anyway, regardless of the polygraph test. Or was he? Ness had something to lose too. His wife and his reputation for a start.

Finally, I told Martin I was ready to take the test. He was very relieved, I could tell. I don't think it ever occurred to Martin I was guilty. He saw this whole thing as something trumped up by Ness and Burton to blackmail him politically before next year's election.

We went back into the living room where Ness and Cowles were sitting. I told them our decision. Martin's and my caveat was that before I did anything, we wanted their solemn word of honor that nothing that happened or was said in the hotel suite would ever be documented in any record or file or ever be discussed with anyone inside or outside the police department. They agreed, but very reluctantly.

Dr. Grossman was in the other bedroom, briefing Keeler and his assistant on the questions to be asked. When I went in for the test, Dr. Grossman left the room and went into the living room with the rest of them. Keeler insisted that nobody but his assistant be in the room with him while they gave me the polygraph test.

The damned polygraph test went very quickly. Keeler fired a barrage of questions at me, one after another. Only yes or no answers were allowed. Things like is my name Frank Sweeney? Am I a physician? Did I know Flo Polillo? Did I kill Flo Polillo? The whole thing didn't take longer than thirty minutes, maybe even twenty. When it was over, Keeler took the results to Ness and Cowles. He didn't say anything to me except that I should stay put. His assistant got an ashtray and a cup of coffee for me.

Some ten minutes later, Keeler was back. We need to do it again, he said. Why? I asked him. Keeler said they weren't sure on a few things and needed to clarify the results they had. My interpretation was that I had bamboozled the damn thing and they were hoping if I took it over, they could catch me in something. I smiled, knowing I had beaten the machine. I remember thinking if

I beat it once, I could beat it again. This time, he changed some of the questions. There were a number of questions about Jenny that Ness must have added. Did I know where Jenny was? Did I kill her? Did I put her body in the Cuyahoga River?

When it was over, Keeler again took the paper with the results and went into the living room. I sat in the bedroom there for almost a half an hour wondering what the hell was going on. Finally, Keeler came in and told me they were finished. His assistant unhooked me from the machine. How'd I do, I asked them both. It depends on your point of view, Keeler said with a poker face. He told me he wasn't able to discuss the results with me.

When I walked into the living room, all the conversation stopped. I seemed to be the catalyst for them to scatter. Everybody was very serious. Martin asked me to go into the bedroom, close the door, and wait for him. I did as he requested. I sat on the bed chain smoking and dying for one small shot of whiskey. Even bad whiskey. Rotgut whiskey. Anything that would dull the frayed endings of my nerves.

A good forty-five minutes later, Martin was back, and Agnes was with him. I had no idea she had been sitting all that time in the hotel coffee shop. Martin had brought her with him when he had come to the hotel that morning. I hugged her and thanked her for coming. My dear Agnes, on whom I can always rely.

We'd better all sit down and figure out what we do next, Martin said gravely. We have a very serious problem to deal with, Frank. You failed the lie detector test both times in a rather spectacular way.

Apparently, Keeler said he'd rarely seen a situation where the person was so clearly lying as I had been. Martin said Dr. Grossman had only compounded the problem by stating that, from the psychiatric profile he had drawn of me, he thought I was very capable of committing the murders.

For the first time since they brought me there, I was getting scared. I felt like I was walking deeper and deeper into a trap. Worst of all, I was helping them trap me. Submitting to that goddamn test. Thinking I could fool the machine. Then letting myself take it again with all those questions about Jenny. The result of it is that now I've really drawn Ness into it personally. Now he knew I killed her.

Martin sat in the armchair talking about lawyers and juries. I didn't really listen closely, and I don't think Agnes did either. Martin was under tremendous pressure, not always making sense as he jumped from one thought to another.

Agnes sat next to me on the bed and put her arms around me. She lay her head on my chest and whispered to me that she would always love me no matter what happened. What a sad and serious expression she had on her face. She looked up into my eyes and asked, Frank, don't you think you'd better tell Martin everything? She didn't want Martin to go on assuming I was innocent.

I looked down into those sad eyes of hers and felt a strange mixture of pain and relief. Relief, because I didn't have to hide it from her anymore. Pain, because I caused her so much sorrow. If there was only some way I could have turned back the clock and lived the past few years of my life over, I would have made Agnes proud of me.

Poor Martin. Sitting there talking with no one listening. He had himself and his family to think about. He had to think of how to control the damage I had created. It would be awful when the press got a hold of it. Martin, I said to him, I don't deserve any more of your help. Think only of yourself and your family and distance yourself from me.

There was a knock on the bedroom door. It was Ness. He wanted to speak to me alone. We went into the other bedroom where he shut the door behind us. Sit down, he ordered. I sat in the armchair while he sat on the bed and lighted a cigarette.

For a minute or longer, he just glared at me. I could feel his hatred penetrating me. Then he spoke in a low voice, so soft I could hardly hear him. His teeth were clenched. Sweeney, he said, I don't know how I'll get you, without destroying everyone around you, but I will get you. You'll pay for this. He just sat there and smoked, not saying another word.

I thought back to last year and the year before. How desperate I was to have him involved with the case. How anxious my big ego was to have him personally acknowledge me through what I'd done. Now that I had so completely achieved that insane goal, I realized it meant the end of me. There was nothing left for me now.

There were only three choices I could see for myself. Suicide was one of them, certainly. I suppose it would have been the honorable thing to do, but it would have brought even greater pain to the only person in the world who loves me.

There was always the option of trying to fight this battle and keep my freedom as long as I could. But because I know I cannot stop myself from killing again, eventually they would get me and execute me. And with me, I'd drag Martin and Agnes and everyone else in my family down in the mud. That was even worse than suicide.

I wasn't sure if the last choice was really open to me. It required agreement from Ness. Look, Eliot, I said to him, I have something to suggest to you. He looked up at me and listened. If I were to commit myself to an institution and never come out again, would that satisfy you? He was quiet for a minute or two. Then he said he'd have to think about it.

While he sat there, I told him why he should agree to my proposal. Even if it didn't give the public a clean solution to the case, at least it brought the killings to an end. It avoided the ugly political battle in which he and Martin would both be damaged in the press. And it kept under wraps the fact we both had a common interest in the same pretty girl.

He got up from the bed and said he wanted to talk about my idea with Cowles. He was gone for quite some time. I lighted cigarette after cigarette while I continued to review my bleak alternatives. When he came back, he had a very solemn expression on his face. Okay, he said. I'll go along with it in principle. You and Cowles work out the details this afternoon, and I'll make a final decision later today when Cowles talks to me.

I was delighted he agreed. Everyone wins this way, I said to him. He shook his head. No, he said with disgust, nobody wins. Fewer people lose. He turned his back on me and left the room. Left me to plan with Cowles my life of confinement.

I went back to Agnes and Martin and told them of the decision. Agnes was so happy. Martin looked confused. I can't say that I blame the poor man. I had dumped a ton of shit on him. I asked him if he would act as my lawyer and work out the details that afternoon with Cowles. He said yes. I could tell he was relieved Ness and I had agreed on the solution we had.

Now that all the drama has died down, I am left with the rest of my life. I have packed up some of my personal things I will not need at the hospital, including this last volume of my journal. Agnes can put my things in the trunks I have in her attic. Tomorrow she and Lee are going to drive me out to Sandusky, my new home. I've given Agnes my car as a present, with the hope she will learn to drive it. Maybe then I will see her more than a few times a year.

Main Characters

Dr. Francis "Frank" Edward Sweeney

Dr. Frank Sweeney, Attribution: Courtesy of Saint Louis University
Libraries Archives & Records Management

DR. SWEENEY WAS BORN IN 1894 into an impoverished Irish immigrant family living on Cleveland's east side in the Kingsbury Run
area. Tragedy marked his life early. His father, Martin J. Sweeney,
was a laborer who had been badly injured in an accident and suffered from tuberculosis, alcoholism, and psychosis. His mother,
Delia O'Mara, died of a heart attack when he was nine. He and his
siblings were left to eke out a very frugal existence.

In 1917, Frank joined the Army and served in France for a couple of years. He suffered a head injury severe enough to receive a monthly benefit for what was termed a 25% disability. Head injuries are notorious for their deleterious effects on personality and behavior and may have been a factor in his severe mental and emotional issues. In fact, head injuries are often diagnosed in serial killers.

Despite his family's poverty, Frank was determined to make a success of himself. His high intelligence and strong work ethic allowed him to work his way through his undergraduate education, pharmacy school, and medical school. Throughout much of his education, he held full-time jobs. His classmates in medical school elected him vice president of his sophomore class and his professors recommended him without reservation.

After decades of exhausting effort, he graduated from St. Louis University School of Medicine in 1928 and became a surgical resident at St. Alexis Hospital in Cleveland. His siblings remembered him as a man who was almost completely absorbed in science and medicine. Even so, he would stop whatever he was doing and immediately attend to a friend or family member who was injured or sick. His concern for the health of his children, his siblings, and their children endeared him to them. They all respected his intelligence and medical expertise.

Dr. Sweeney's expertise as a surgical resident allowed him to become a protégé of Dr. Carl Hamann, the highly respected teaching physician. Sweeney seemed to have a very promising life ahead of him. He had married Mary Sokol, a dark-haired Slavic beauty, and had two young sons. The many years of hardship and deprivation were becoming distant memories for him and his young family.

Unfortunately, just on the eve of his hard-earned achievements, destructive pressures were building inside of him. Overwork and a hereditary tendency toward alcoholism and psychosis began to take an obvious toll on him. He was admitted to City Hospital for alcoholism, but the treatment was unsuccessful. The drinking worsened, and his marriage and career began to disintegrate. He was violent and abusive at home, and the hospital severed its relationship with him. Eventually, his wife filed for divorce in 1936, seeking custody of the children and an order restraining him from "visiting, interfering, or molesting her."

According to his wife, Dr. Sweeney had begun to drink continuously two years after their marriage in July of 1927. She said he remained in a state of habitual drunkenness until their separation. The timing of Dr. Sweeney's deterioration seemed to reach a climax around the time that the so-called "Lady of the Lake," the likely first victim in the murder series, washed up on the shores of Lake Erie.

In the mid-to-late 1930s, Dr. Sweeney spent time in the Sandusky, Ohio, veterans hospital, allegedly to treat his alcoholism. In March of 1938, a dog found an expertly amputated leg nearby that could not be attributed to legitimate surgery in any area hospital or any missing persons report. This event focused investigators on Dr. Sweeney, who were aware of his frequent trips to the veterans hospital in recent years. From mid-1938, Dr. Sweeney spent most of his time in various veterans hospitals, eventually spending the last part of his life in the hospital in Dayton. There was a period in the mid-1950s that he wrote at least five bizarre, incoherent postcards and a letter to Eliot Ness.

On one of the postcards, Dr. Sweeney attaches what appears to be the front of a flower seed packet with a large pansy and this message:

To: Eliot 'AM BIG U ous NESS' UNION COMMERCE BUILDING CLEVELAND OHIO U.S.A.

[Vertically, next to pansy flower:]
WITH THE ADVENT OF SPRING, THE APIS APIDAE WILL AGAIN GATHER THE PRECIOUS NECTAR FROM YE OLDE CURIOSITY LOCUS

[Below pansy seed packet:]
N.B. NOTHING XPLOSIVE HERIN [sic]

[At top, left of stamp:]
Good Cheer
The American Sweeney

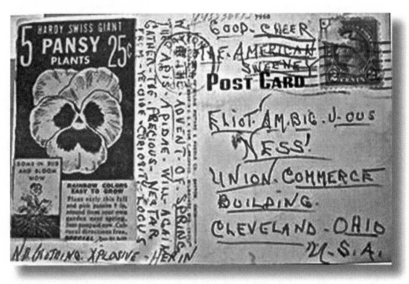

Sweeney postcard
Attribution: The Western Reserve Historical Society, Cleveland, Ohio

On another equally incoherent postcard, there is what appears to be a description of a book titled *Handbook for Poisoners*. On this postcard, he calls himself F.E. Sweeney M.D. Paranoidal Nemesis.

His medical records at this time indicate he believed the hospital was trying to poison him.

Aside from a period in the middle of the 1950s, Dr. Sweeney wrote perfectly coherent letters, several of which were regarding his applications to hospitals seeking a position on their medical staff. The hospitals he contacted assumed that Dr. Sweeney was on the staff of the Dayton veterans hospital, not a patient. He died in 1964.

Alcoholism, drug dependency, and mental deterioration made Dr. Sweeney a compelling suspect, plus the fact that he lived in the Kingsbury Run area for much of his life. He knew the savage ravine intimately from his boyhood explorations. Dr. Sweeney was tall and very strong, powerful enough to carry the first two victims down the steep, ragged embankment of Jackass Hill in Kingsbury Run in pitch dark. Clearly, he had the medical knowledge to perform so many expert decapitations and dismemberments. Finally, Dr. Sweeney's alleged bisexuality could possibly explain why the Mad Butcher chose male and female victims. Most serial killers focus on one sex or the other.

AGNES SWEENEY BALDWIN

Agnes, Dr. Sweeney's beloved sister, was the youngest of six children. She was born in 1897 and died in 1982. She dropped out of school in the fifth grade to make money to help support the family. Working downtown in various stores, she walked home in the dark to East 71st Street to save a fare of three cents. There was only one tavern after E. 14th Street that had any street lighting.

She learned bookkeeping and rose in that field to become the Senior Bookkeeper for White Motor Company. She married Leland S Baldwin, a mechanical engineer, in 1924 when she was twenty-seven. They had one child, Patricia.

PATRICIA BALDWIN KILPATRICK

Patricia, the daughter of Leland and Agnes Baldwin, was born in 1927 and died March 3, 2016. She was inspired by her mother's drive and ambition to work her way through the business world without a formal education. Patricia earned a Master's Degree at Case Western Reserve University. She was appointed Dean of CWRU's Flora Stone Mather College and over the years earned increasingly higher posts in the university. She became the first woman named Vice President of Case Western Reserve University.

CONGRESSMAN MARTIN L. SWEENEY

CONGRESSMAN MARTIN L. SWEENEY,
Attribution: United States Library of Congress's Prints and
Photographs division, *Harris & Ewing* collection

Martin L. was the first cousin of Dr. Frank Sweeney. His parents were Dominic Sweeney and Ann Cleary Sweeney. He was a Cleveland municipal court judge for more than a decade. He was elected to serve in the Seventy-second Congress to fill a vacancy and continued to serve until 1943.

Martin L. was a dedicated Democrat and an outspoken critic of Republican Mayor Harold H. Burton and his Director of Public Safety, Eliot Ness.

ELIOT NESS

ELIOT NESS
Attribution: Public domain image
courtesy of WikiMedia Commons

After his success in fighting the Capone Mob in Chicago, Ness became head of the police and fire departments in Cleveland, Ohio. He transformed a corrupt and incompetent police force into a modern model for the country. His contributions to Cleveland's safety forces were the pinnacle of his career.

Later, he became the chairman of Diebold Corporation. Subsequent business ventures did not fare as well. In a lapse of judgment, he was persuaded to run in an unsuccessful bid for mayor of

Cleveland as an independent against a popular Democratic incumbent. He, his third wife, Betty Andersen Ness, and his adopted son, Bobby, led a humble existence in Coudersport, PA until his death on May 16, 1957, of a heart attack.

LIEUTENANT DAVID L. COWLES

Lt David L. Cowles,
Attribution: *Cleveland Press* Archives, Cleveland State University

Cowles was a highly intelligent man who was self-educated in scientific methods. He was the head of the Scientific Investigation Bureau, the formal name of the Cleveland Police Department crime laboratory, and a respected confidant of Eliot Ness.

CORONER SAMUEL R. GERBER

Dr. Samuel Gerber,
Attribution: *Cleveland Press* Archives, Cleveland State University

Dr. Gerber was elected Cuyahoga County coroner in 1937 and remained in that position until 1986. He was preceded in office by Coroner Pearse.

DR. ROYAL GROSSMAN

Dr. Grossman was a Cleveland physician who was the court psychiatrist for Cuyahoga County.

LEONARDE KEELER

Leonarde Keeler was the co-inventor of the polygraph, better known as the lie detector. At the request of Eliot Ness, he brought the latest version of his polygraph with him on his way from Chicago to Cleveland to test Dr. Frank Sweeney in 1938. At that time, the only polygraph in the Cleveland area was in the city of East Cleveland. Ness would not have been able to use the East Cleveland polygraph and still ensure the confidentiality of his investigation of Dr. Sweeney.

THOMAS WHELAN

Whelan was a police officer assigned to follow Dr. Sweeney. Later, Whelan became an attorney.

Discovery of the American Sweeney Todd's Identity

IT WAS A SECRET ELIOT NESS and a handful of confidantes kept for more than thirty years: the solution to one of the most horrific serial murder cases ever recorded at that time. Had the secret endured for much longer, it most likely would have remained a secret today. Why? Because the handful of people who knew the identity of the killer would all be long dead.

When I was a fifth grader at Miles Elementary School in Cleveland, I went with my classmate Barbara to her house after school. Immediately, I called my mother to tell her, and she asked where Barbara lived. Kingsbury Run I said.

"You have to come home right now," she said, her voice bordering on hysteria. I don't recall the exact words that tumbled out of her mouth, but they included "murder" and "headless." I offered to take the bus back to my house, but my mother wouldn't hear of it. It was too dangerous, she told me. She insisted on talking to Barbara's mother, who reluctantly agreed to wake her husband, who worked the night shift, to drive me across the city to my home. It was a very quiet, awkward ride. When I got home, my mother told me that terrible murders happened in Kingsbury Run and that I should never go there.

That fleeting memory of Kingsbury Run remained dormant in my mind for decades. Fast forward to the 1970s. Walter Bell, my husband at that time, and I dabbled in writing stories when we came home from work. One of our ideas—the story of a bloody revolution in America by the Weather Underground—got the attention of a producer for the ABC *Movie of the Week*. The producer urged us to pitch ideas that weren't violent like the one we had submitted.

It was then that my fifth-grade memory of Kingsbury Run firmly re-emerged and established itself in the forefront of my mind. I learned that in the thirties, a dozen or more gruesome decapitation murders took place in Kingsbury Run. During that period, the legendary Eliot Ness was in charge of the police force and fire department. Twelve murders and possibly even thirteen that even Eliot Ness couldn't solve? There were almost three times as many victims as Jack the Ripper's five prostitutes.

Walter repeatedly reasoned with me to forget about this case and think about story ideas that were not violent. There was no way that ABC's *Movie of the Week* would accept a pitch about a serial killer that decapitated his victims. He was right, of course, but I couldn't let it go. I was hooked.

Months later, Walter and I visited his friend's new playhouse in the Flats, the steel mill and warehouse district on the Cuyahoga River. I happened to mention to the theater's owner that I thought the theater patio was near one of the places that a victim of the so-called "Mad Butcher of Kingsbury Run" had been discovered. We discussed how spooky it would be to have a play about the murders on the theater's patio. Walter and I talked about writing the play, but didn't make any headway on it, mostly because we didn't have any idea at that time what kind of person the killer was.

We were surprised much later when the *Cleveland Press* had a feature article about the play we had supposedly written which was going to be performed at the theater in the Flats. We never did write the play, but the article resulted in a very important phone call.

Dr. Royal Grossman, the former Cuyahoga County court psychiatrist, told me that he was involved when Eliot Ness solved the case in a secret meeting. He explained that Ness had the killer confined to a veterans hospital in 1938. Dr. Grossman refused to divulge the killer's name because Ness had made the few people who knew the killer's identity swear they would keep it secret. The doctor offered to give us the details of the meeting if we learned the killer's identity. Now, at least, we knew why the murders stopped in 1938.

I had also tracked David L. Cowles, the former head of the police crime lab, to where he was living in Florida. In our telephone call, he confirmed Dr. Grossman's story but also refused to divulge the name of the man he and Eliot Ness believed to be the Kingsbury Run killer.

We had already collected a great deal of information on the case from the local newspapers and had written several chapters of a novel when we learned that our typist's home had been broken into and the manuscript was the only item that was stolen. The event was at once frightening and annoying. Frightening because someone seemed to have us under surveillance and would break the law to learn what we were writing. Annoying because the stolen papers were our only copy of the manuscript and Walter wasn't willing to spend any more time on projects that wouldn't be appropriate for the ABC *Movie of the Week*.

I had an idea that I hoped would yield more information about who Eliot Ness determined was the killer and, at the same time, renew Walter's interest in the case. I put an ad in the "Personals" section of the *Cleveland Plain Dealer* that read "ANYONE having evidence to convict Kingsbury Run Murderer, please call Walter

Bell." and provided—without his knowledge—his office number at Cuyahoga Community College. The next day, I could hardly keep my mind on my work and was disappointed that Walter hadn't called about the ad that had been running since the morning. I assumed that no one had called about the ad. When he came home after work, he said, "Oh, by the way, the only call I got from your ad was a *Plain Dealer* reporter. He wants to interview us tomorrow morning."

I was thrilled. An article appeared on the back of the first section of the newspaper the next day. A couple days later, my close friend Georgiana and I went out to celebrate at an upscale restaurant and bar in Shaker Square. We sat for a while in the small bar when I noticed an older man enter the bar and sit directly across from us. His demeanor and clothing seemed out of place for the sophisticated restaurant. He stared at us continuously, making us nervous about staying there.

Georgiana suggested that we leave and go to a restaurant in Mayfield Heights that had a band. The Mayfield Heights restaurant was virtually empty when we arrived around eight o'clock because the band didn't start until nine. We sat at the empty bar and ordered drinks. Shortly afterward, the bartender answered the phone at the bar, looked over at us, said something, and hung up. He immediately brought each of us two free drinks. We mistakenly assumed that he was giving us free drinks to keep us there so the establishment wouldn't appear so empty.

Some twenty minutes later, a well-dressed man in a suit who appeared to be in his thirties came into the restaurant and sat next to me at the bar. I figured this man was looking for female companionship and turned toward my friend, with my back to the stranger.

"You look familiar," he said in a friendly tone. "Weren't you in the newspaper a few days ago?"

I agreed, but it troubled me that only my husband's photo was in the article, not mine. I was beginning to understand I was being followed. The next thing he asked was why I was interested in a case from the thirties. I explained that my husband and I were going to write a book and a screenplay that would reveal the new information we had learned.

Then, his expression became considerably less friendly. "Are the Republicans putting you up to this?"

I had no idea what he was talking about and told him so, but he didn't believe me.

"You don't fool around with Bob Sweeney and get away with it. My advice to you is to drop it before you're sorry. You could just disappear one day."

That said, he paid for our drinks and left the restaurant. I figured the man who stared at us in the Shaker Heights restaurant was also connected with this Bob Sweeney as well. But who was Bob Sweeney and what was his problem with "the Republicans?" And more importantly, why was he having me followed?

We learned that Robert E. Sweeney was a prominent Democratic politician and attorney. He was the son of the powerful Congressman Martin L. Sweeney, who was a major critic of Eliot Ness and the Republican mayor who had hired Ness. What we didn't know was how he was connected to the case.

We also received calls from Tommy Whelan, an attorney who had been a cop during the 1930s, and then Dr. Hosler, a friend of Ness. Both men also confirmed Dr. Grossman's story of the secret meeting and like Grossman, had been sworn to secrecy about the identity of the killer. However, Whelan and Hosler agreed to tell us the details if we learned the secret identity of the killer.

At some point, Walter received a call from Alex Archaki, a former burglar, who said he knew who the serial killer was. He wanted to meet with us late one rainy night at a bar on the Case Western Reserve campus. Archaki had a shotgun concealed under his raincoat, concerned that he might be attacked for revealing what he knew.

We learned soon enough from the meeting with Archaki that Dr. Francis Edward Sweeney was the first cousin of Congressman Martin L. Sweeney and Robert Sweeney was Martin's son. Archaki said that the Sandusky, Ohio, veterans hospital shared grounds with the Ohio Penitentiary Honor Farm, which is how he met Dr. Sweeney. He and the doctor had a symbiotic relationship: Sweeney would write barbiturate prescriptions for Archaki, and Archaki would get liquor for Sweeney.

When the murder victims started to appear in Kingsbury Run, the coroner and forensic autopsy surgeons believed that the killer was likely either a doctor, male nurse, or possibly even a hunter. The decapitations and other dissections showed a clear under-standing of the human body. Consequently, detectives focused on area doctors, male nurses, undertakers, and hunters. Archaki noticed that sometimes Dr. Sweeney would be at the VA hospital in the timeframe police estimated a murder had occurred but couldn't be located during the time he was supposedly in residence there. Upon two occasions at least, Archaki recalled that Dr. Sweeney had driven to the Sandusky hospital and then disappeared for a day or two before returning, without checking himself out of the hospital. Subsequently, when I contacted the VA hospital, an administrator said that Dr. Sweeney's record had a note to call the Cleveland Police chief if he left the grounds.

Betty Andersen Ness, Eliot's third wife and widow, was another valuable source. She was living in California when I called her. She laughed when I mentioned Dr. Sweeney. "He used to get drunk and call Eliot frequently at his office to taunt him," she said. He'd tell Eliot things that only the killer could know." There was no doubt in her mind or her husband's that the doctor was guilty of the Kingsbury Run murders.

Now that we were certain we had the name of the key suspect, we called back Dr. Grossman, Dr. Hosler, and Tommy Whelan, all of whom confirmed the identity of Dr. Frank Sweeney. When I contacted David Cowles, he angrily demanded to know who had given me that name and, because I didn't reveal my sources, he slammed the phone down.

We asked Mrs. Ness, Dr. Grossman, and Tommy Whelan why Ness didn't prosecute Dr. Sweeney. They said that Ness simply didn't have any physical evidence to convict Dr. Sweeney. There were two other circumstances Ness considered. Congressman Martin L. Sweeney was a vocal critic of Ness and Mayor Harold Burton's administration. Ness and Mayor Burton weren't going to take on a powerful enemy with so little chance of a conviction. Additionally, Sweeney's siblings were decent, hardworking people who didn't deserve to be linked to the terrible crimes of their brother.

As I gathered reams of documents about Dr. Sweeney: his medical and court records, his correspondence with the FBI, the threats to my safety continued, even at my place of work. I was the editor of five business reference publications for Predicasts, Inc. at University Circle. One of the publications focused on international industries and companies.

An important component of that publication was content from German business journals, and my German language expert had just graduated from college and moved away. For more than a month, the German newspapers piled up and then I thought I got lucky. A very distinguished attorney in his sixties came to my office.

He was fluent in German, having been born and raised there. He said he had practiced trial law in Cleveland until he had a heart attack and could not risk the stress of continuing that line of work. He offered to abstract the German publications for no compensation other than having "something interesting and useful" to do with his time.

He often asked me about what I had learned in my investigation. This went on for several months until one day he told me he had to resign. He was going to work for Bob Sweeney. When I accused him of working for Bob Sweeney all along, he offered me a sincere warning. "You're a nice girl," he said. "You need to drop this investigation right now. You have no idea what can happen to you. They'll never even find your body."

At this point in time, Walter was working downtown with Channel 5's eleven o'clock news team and didn't get home until after one a.m. Alone in a big old house in Cleveland Heights that seemed to me to creak and groan every night. Alone with seven children—his, mine, and ours—I would get phone calls with threats and calls after midnight where no one would speak. I was truly frightened for myself and the children.

Walter called the Cleveland Heights police every time there was a threat. Then, for a couple of hours that night, there would be a police car outside the house. One of the detectives listened to our belief as to the source of the threats. "They don't want you to reveal Dr. Sweeney's name because it could damage Bob Sweeney's political goals. So why doesn't Walter, since he works at Channel 5, get the people there to let him tell the audience what you found out about Dr. Sweeney. That way, if anything happens to you, we'll go after Bob Sweeney.

Walter did what the officer suggested and announced what we had learned about Dr. Frank Sweeney. The following night on

Channel 5, a family member claimed that Bob Sweeney wasn't related to Dr. Sweeney, even though we had all the birth and death certificates to prove it. It was a sensible suggestion, and it worked. There were no more threats.

When our research into the Kingsbury Run murders was completed in the seventies, we had planned to write a nonfiction book on that subject, having collected so much research on the case. We never did. Walter and I had both remarried, and I had moved to northern Virginia. Over time, I had worked my way up to an executive in the blossoming Internet business. In my spare time, I started the Crime Library website, hiring detectives, law librarians, crime reporters, profilers, and forensic professors to write informative stories about major crimes, trials, and forensic science.

Many of the stories on serial killers, I wrote myself. I had also written the journals of the American Sweeney Todd. In 2000, Time Warner's Court TV bought the rights to the Crime Library and hired me to expand and manage it.

Suddenly, I had the means to grow the Crime Library into the premier true crime website on the Net. Coincidentally, somewhat earlier, my dear friend, James Jessen Badal, and I were looking to Kent State University Press to publish the nonfiction book.

It would have been impossible for me to find adequate time to manage and grow the Crime Library website and work with Jim on the nonfiction book. So, I made sure Jim had all my research. He is a tenacious and highly talented sleuth who greatly expanded my research on the Kingsbury Run murders and other similar cases. Consequently, his books are the most comprehensive source for the Cleveland Torso murders. I highly recommend James Jessen Badal's books on the Torso Murders. *In the Wake of the Butcher: Cleveland Torso Murders, Authoritative Edition, Revised and*

Expanded (Black Squirrel Books 2014). This is the most detailed and authoritative book on the murders.

Though Murder Has No Tongue: The Lost Victim of Cleveland's Mad Butcher (Black Squirrel Books 2010) thoroughly analyzes the tragedy of a suspect arrested for the murders who never saw freedom again.

Hell's Wasteland: The Pennsylvania Torso Murders (Black Squirrel Books 2013) evaluates the evidence on whether the Mad Butcher of Cleveland also killed in Pennsylvania.

Photo Gallery

Edward Andrassy: Attribution: Mugshot, Courtesy of the Cleveland Police Department

Florence (Flo) Polillo Mugshot, Courtesy of the Cleveland Police Department

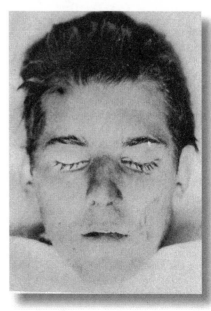

Caption: The Tattooed Man, Victim Number 4, morgue photo (Morgue photos are also public records i.e. public domain)

Eliot Ness questions hobos in Kingsbury Run,
Attribution: *Cleveland Press* Archives,
Cleveland State University

Police drag for victims in Kingsbury Run, Attribution:
Cleveland Press Archives, Cleveland State University

Hobos in Kingsbury Run, Attribution: *Cleveland Press*
Archives, Cleveland State University

Proof

Made in the USA
Charleston, SC
31 January 2017